Born in 1942 in the form

Kerala, **M. Mukundan** is

India Today. Author of twe.

collections of short stories, a play and a study on ...

his best-selling books include *On the Banks of the Mayyazhi, Kesavan's Lamentations, Delhi, Dance and God's Mischief* for which he won the Sahitya Akademi Award. A leading pioneer of high modernism in Malayalam fiction, Mukundan has won several other prestigious awards including the Vayalar Award, and the first Crossword Award for Indian language fiction in English translation (*Mayyazhipuzhayude Theerangalil*, translated into English as *On the Banks of the Mayyazhi*) and honours including Chevalier of Arts and Letters from the French Government.

A.J. Thomas has translated extensively from Malayalam poetry, fiction and drama. He is the recipient of the Katha Award and the AKMG Prize.

Kesavan's Lamentations

A Novel

M. Mukundan

Translated by

A.J. Thomas

Rupa . Co

Published 2006 by
Rupa . Co
7/16, Ansari Road, Daryaganj,
New Delhi 110 002

Sales Centres:

Allahabad Bangalore Chandigarh Chennai
Hyderabad Jaipur Kathmandu
Kolkata Mumbai Pune

Typeset in Nikita Overseas Pvt. Ltd.
1410 Chiranjiv Tower
43 Nehru Place
New Delhi 110 019

Printed in India by
Gopsons Papers Ltd.
A-14, Sector-60
Noida 201 301

To

EMS,

who lives on...

Preface

The Real and the Mythical

Kesavante Vilapangal — translated here as Kesavan's Lamentations — is an intensely political novel. As evident from his earlier novels, Mukundan, one of the progenitors of modernity in Malayalam literature, has been sensitive to the people's struggle for liberation from colonial domination, the post-colonial disappointments and frustration, and the brutalisation that slowly set in, in Indian society. Thematic novelty and innovative craft are the hallmarks of his earlier works, which have earned him much literary recognition and acclaim. *Kesavante Vilapangal,* in a sense, is a continuation of his earlier works, yet different in both conception and narrative strategy.

The formation and articulation of the Left political consciousness in Kerala forms the central theme of the novel, whose focus is on E.M.S. Namboodiripad, who, arguably, exercised the most decisive influence on its course. Yet this is not a work on or about EMS, even if the novel revolves around him. It is neither a biographical account of EMS nor a representation, faithful or otherwise, of his social and political activism. The novel therefore escapes being a caricature of EMS, as in Arundhati Roy's *The God of Small Things* or in some Malayalam literary resurrections after his death. At the same time, the presence of EMS in the novel is overarching, almost divine and mythical, which mediates at every stage, decisively influencing its course.

Kesavante Vilapangal has a multi-layered structure with a complex narrative strategy that brings out a relationship, almost symbiotic in nature, between its two main strands. There are, in fact, two intertwined and complementary plots in the novel. The first is about the tensions and travails as well as the popular recognition involved in the production of a literary work, drawing upon contemporary political issues and leaders. This is exemplified by the experience of the protagonist of the novel, Kesavan, a fairly successful writer, who undertakes to compose a novel on EMS. The second is the novel so written by Kesavan in which EMS looms large through a mythic presence in the life of a boy named Appukuttan. In the course of the narrative the distinction between the narrator and the narrated is so blurred that the former becomes a victim of the fallout of his own creative effort.

The myth takes shape in the life of Appukuttan while he was still in the cradle. Its beginning is marked by the inexplicable influence on the boy exercised by a photograph of EMS fixed on the wall by Appukuttan's uncle. He grows up in its enchanting presence and is enamoured of the leader's childlike smile and the red colour that embellished the portrait's background. The child, it appeared, was in constant communication with the photograph, so much so that he protested when his view was obstructed by a change in the position of the cradle. In due course the myth assumes dynamic qualities, directing the mental and physical world of the child. In a crowded fair he could, even when he was only three years old, lead his father to the place where the photograph of EMS was on sale along with those of innumerable gods and goddesses. Or is it that the photograph was drawing him towards it? The influence thus exercised was so overpowering that the child in Appukuttan was marginalised; he did not enjoy the company of his friends, nor indulge in what children are normally fond of. His world was confined to EMS and to the possibilities inherent in the ideas that he represented. His sole ambition was to pursue the path charted out by EMS and to end up as a martyr for that cause. As a result he sought to fashion himself in the image of EMS, meticulously tried to follow and internalise the details of his life, and to devote himself to the pursuit of the ideals set by him. Yet, EMS remained enigmatic and mythical — distant but intimate, elusive but accessible, and awe-inspiring but gentle. He had no opportunity to know the 'real' EMS — Mukundan's engagement is not with the real — but the myth is so firmly embedded in his mind that he effortlessly translates it into real politics.

The translation of the myth into the reality of politics is facilitated by the mediation of his schoolteacher, Aman Master, who transforms Appukuttan from a dull and indifferent student to a front-runner in the class. Aman Master envisions in him a future leader and, reminiscent of the role school teachers have played in the dissemination of Left influence in Kerala, guides him in that direction. To the dismay of his father, a disillusioned

Naxalite who sought solace in religion, Appukuttan, though only fifteen years old, associates himself with the Communist Party. His ambition always was to become a martyr, which he ultimately becomes by killing another former Naxalite who had turned an alcoholic and committed the 'sacrilege' of urinating on a photograph of EMS. Appukuttan is arrested and taken to jail where he finds fulfilment in the strong arms of EMS who descends from a red star in the sky surrounded by a red halo. Thus Kesavan's political choice is clearly delineated.

Kesavan's attempt to construct the myth of EMS elicits a variety of responses. A Left-leaning intellectual and literary critic warns him that writing on a theme that he is ignorant of is short of serious danger. That he buttresses his arguments with quotations from *Living in Truth* by Vaclav Havel and *Reality Effect* by Ronald Barthes is possibly intended as a comment on the intellectual practice in Kerala.

However, when the novel was completed, the same critic writes a laudatory review and also offers to use his political influence to get Kesavan important positions in government-controlled academies. He also receives a lucrative offer from a commercial publisher. All of these Kesavan rejects with disdain. To him, the moment of fulfilment was beyond all these, when the myth he created turns real and EMS appears in person before him, though for a fleeting moment, to bless him and thus give recognition to his creative ability.

The opposition to and disapproval of Kesavan's work were equally sharp. They presumably came from the Hindu fundamentalist groups which sent him anonymous letters threatening him for writing on the present-day Sankaran and not on Adi Sankara. This is reminiscent of the tactics of Hindu communalists who threaten and intimidate the secular intelligentsia who are critical of their cultural and political projects. Kesavan ignored the threats and publicly denounces them, which lead to his murder. The novel thus ends by underlying the ominous possibilities inherent in Hindu fundamentalism.

The Left intellectual and political life in Kerala was largely dependent upon the theoretical erudition and political acumen of EMS. For a long time he strode like a colossus, guiding and influencing its direction. EMS was not only a leader engaged in everyday politics, but was an effective communicator who took great care to disseminate his ideas in society and thus to intervene in the existing social and political consciousness and eventually to transform them. The myth that the novel so cleverly creates is actually a reflection of this reality. But then the foregrounding of the myth is in itself an attempt to explore the meaning of the real. The subtle and suggestive manner in which the novel underlines the relationship between the real and the mythic makes it an extremely complex work, compelling a critical introspection on how political ideals make or unmake popular consciousness.

K.N. Panikkar

Frontline, September 10, 1999

One

His father called him Appu. His mother called him Kuttan. And the people... Appukkuttan. Thus, it is the people who made him complete...

Kesavan begins his new novel thus. This is his fourth novel. And his eleventh book.

After writing this much, he sits up, straightening himself in the chair, contemplating the lines he has written in red ink on white paper. Although Kesavan's handwriting is neat, as he writes, his lines tend to droop and go aslant. Presently, a doubt assails him. Isn't the sentence 'Thus, it is the people who made him complete...' redundant? Even without the benefit of that sentence, the meaning he intended was already clear.

Kesavan picks up the pen to write the next sentence. It was a fountain pen filled with ink. He detests ballpoint pens. Kesavan believes that the ballpoint pen, which facilitates smooth writing, is meant for writers of pulp fiction. He likes writing in fits and starts. That's why he shudders when he hears that some people compose novels on the computer. Ravunni, the historian and literary critic, once told Kesavan: 'You haven't yet begun to make preparations for the future; you lag far behind the others.'

Presently, Kesavan felt like spitting. Putting the pen down on the table, he went over to the window and spat out with a long-drawn hawk. Hearing the commotion, a mother hen in the yard hurriedly tucked her brood under her wings.

'Hey, what're you doing?' He looked kitchenwards.

'I'm straining water from the rice.'

'Come for a second!'

'What for?'

'To scratch my back...'

Sujatha knows that Kesavan feels many such urges while writing. He would spit often. Scratch his back. Urinate. But when not writing... he is a harmless soul.

'Hey, are you coming or not?'

'The rice will overcook...'

'Damn your rice!'

He tried to scratch his back himself, inserting Sujatha's long-handled comb between his back and his vest. When there were so many man-made inventions around—for grinding, washing clothes, even for measuring blood pressure—how come nobody had invented a machine for scratching one's back?

The hen and her brood were there just below the window. If he so much as spat out noisily, she would tuck her young ones under her wings. And what about the rooster? To find out, he spat out noisily once again. The chicks didn't budge. Could they have lost their reflexes so soon? The rooster casually glanced up once at the sleepy face that appeared at the window.

'Could you grate some coconut for me?' It was Sujatha from the kitchen.

'Do you know who you are asking? The Akademi Award and Vayalar Award winner...!'

'But you haven't got the Muttathu Varkey Award yet...'

'Can one be called a writer only then...?'

'Nor the Ankanam Award...'

'That's not my fault. I am past the age of forty. Can I turn any younger, just to become eligible for that award?'

'Let them give it to me. Aren't I young?'

'What for? Cooking rice?' Quipping thus, Kesavan came back to his table and sat down. 'Hey, why are you glum...?'

'Don't think that I'll spend my days in this kitchen cooking for you. I will step out into the world one day...!'

At that, Kesavan began to laugh.

Unscrewing the pen's cap, he contemplated the nib. Watching him stare thus, one would think that the nib was faulty in some way. After sitting in this manner for some time, he got up and walked over to the verandah. He walked quickly, as if someone had called out to him. The hen and her brood were pacing the yard now, pecking at tidbits here and there. Now there was a crow too, for company. Kesavan adores crows—maybe because the crow is a bird of the masses. He hitched his mundu above his knees and sat down under the eaves. Kesavan has long arms and legs; even his toes are curled up because they are too long. But he wasn't the tallest man in that area. That distinction went to Moosath of the Matham.

Sitting there, Kesavan can see the people who pass through the lane beyond the fence. Most of the time, he can see only their heads because the lane is so sunken. He enjoys seeing people without their torsos. But whenever Moosath of the Matham came along, he saw not only his head but his chest as well. Moosath was the tallest man around. Then again, how was it when Visalakshi Ezhuthamma came that way? Not even her head could be seen. Kesavan would not realise that she had passed by. Ezhuthamma was very short. Moosath must have stolen her height. Kesavan wouldn't know if children and cattle passed through the lane either.

'I am going for my bath,' called out Sujatha. 'Do you want tea?'

'No, I don't.'

'Now, when I am inside the bathroom and have bolted the door, don't call out to me and say 'Hey, enough of your bath, come and make tea for me, quick!' Do you hear?'

'Yes, I do.'

Sujatha was under the impression that her husband was mulling over his novel, sitting in the verandah. But at that moment, neither his novel nor its characters, EMS and Appukkuttan, were anywhere in Kesavan's head. He was counting the heads of those who were passing along the lane. No one could predict the turn Kesavan's thoughts would take. Not even Sujatha, who had lived with him for so long.

Let alone his thoughts, even his look would mislead others. When he looked at Moosath's face, it would be Visalakshi Ezhuthamma's face that he saw. It was his habit to see dwarfish people in tall ones.

When he was tired of sitting in the verandah, he walked over to the gate. Just then, Moosath appeared with a bottle of Horlicks wrapped in paper. He was on his way back from the grocery shop at the Junction.

'What! Didn't you go to the office today?'

'I'm on leave.'

'Anything special? Why are you always on leave?'

'Oh, just like that...'

Why should he tell Moosath that he had availed of leave to write the novel? Moosath didn't seem to be interested in reading novels anyway. Every day, he could be seen passing along the lane at least ten times. Kesavan is interested only in such traffic, but didn't know where Moosath was headed.

Kesavan stood by the gate for some more time, exchanging pleasantries with passers-by. After some time, the length of the shadow of the fence that lay over the compound gradually receded. In the afternoon, this shadow would cross the fence itself and pass onto the lane outside.

Kesavan was bored. Compelling himself to think about something, he decided to chew the cud about some women he knew. Soon, he got back into the house, put on his shirt and went out. He used to go for long walks. There were occasions when he would walk even up to the jetty in the town, which was full of godowns. But after seeing G. Aravindan's film *Pokkuveyil*, in which the protagonist was given to seemingly endless strolling around, Kesavan had developed an intense dislike for walks. Like Moosath had stolen Visalakshi Ezhuthamma's height, Aravindan had stolen the walks of all others and given them to the characters in the film.

Nanootti's shop stood on the main road, by the bus stop. Though his was a paan shop, Nanootti's main wares were soda and sarsaparilla sherbet. There were clusters of people around the shop, as usual. Some waiting for buses, and others just hanging around.

'Didn't you go to the office, today?' Nanootti asked him.

'I am on leave.'

Fortunately, Nanootti didn't question him any further. Kesavan chewed a strong paan with tobacco. He chatted and joked with those who were waiting for the bus. As the Fast Passenger Bus to Payyanur sped by, he returned home with bright, reddened lips, as if he had put on lipstick. Because of the strong tobacco and the heat of the sun, he felt drowsy as he walked along. In fact, he walked into the house asleep.

Satheesan had come back from school. He had classes only till noon because they had a shift system in the school. Sujatha was bathing him in the open, near the well. He had not been given a bath before going to school in the morning because it had been cold. He would catch a cold at the slightest chill and then turtle doves would begin cooing inside his chest.

'This boy's hair is caked with mud. Bathing him is more difficult than bathing an elephant!'

'Isn't he twelve? Let him bathe by himself.'

'I won't take a bath by myself! Our neighbour Pradeep is fourteen, yet his elder sister bathes him. Mother must bathe me!' Satheesan jumped up and down, eyes smarting from the soap lather, and Sujatha whacked him once across his bum.

Kesavan stood watching her hands and bare, wet calves, visible because she had hitched up her sari. Meanwhile, thoughts about EMS entered his head along with the noon breeze. Just as Moosath wasn't interested in reading novels, now he wasn't interested in writing them. To sit under the eaves, with mundu hitched up above the knees; to wear a shirt, go to the Junction and have a fine paan with strong tobacco; to stand in front of Nanootti's shop and chat with acquaintances...Kesavan was interested only in such things now.

Sujatha ladled out rice for Kesavan and Satheesan, who had come in after his bath. Because he was on long leave and at home, she had made erisserry and banana-flower thoran. And curried buttermilk. He mixed the buttermilk into the hot rice and ate, savouring the tasty combination. He would eat lunch from a local restaurant on the days he went to office or share the rice and curry brought by his colleagues from their homes. His friends would vie with each other in offering him their lunches. His fame as a writer prompted all this.

After drinking some chukkuvellam, he came back to the verandah and stood there. The heads that had bobbed above the fence were not to be seen anymore. Who would venture out in this high noon, in the scorching sun? The midday has its own peculiar silence, thought Kesavan—different from the silences of midnight and dawn.

'Is your work over?'

'Why?'

'Let's lie down for a while.'

'I have some sewing to do.'

'It was a mistake to buy you a sewing machine. Nowadays I can't get you even for a minute.'

'*You* didn't buy this machine for me. Didn't I buy it with my own money? With the money from the chit fund...'

'Where did you get the money to join the chit fund and maintain it?'

'My husband gave it to me!'

They laughed together. If the photographer of some weekly magazine had seen that scene, he would have promptly snapped away. The happy family of the novelist.

Kesavan took off his vest and hung it on a nail on the wall. Then he opened the window and stretched himself out on the bed. Lying there, he could see the pepper vines that had climbed and spread themselves around the murikku tree. In his childhood, whenever he caught a cold, his mother would boil some water with crushed pepper and add a lump of jaggery for him to drink, Kesavan remembered. A crow cawed, marking time with the rhythm of the noontime silence. Presently, the clatter of Sujatha's sewing machine rose.

Kesavan's eyes slowly closed as he lay with his hands folded over his chest. He could not hear the din of Sujatha's sewing machine now. Instead, he would recognise it as the rattle of a metre-gauge train that climbed up along mountainous tracks in some distant, unknown land. After some time, he woke up, perspiring all over, as if he had taken a Paracetamol for a fever. He got up drowsily, went over to the table and wrote, his eyes barely half open.

Appukkuttan's gaze, while lying in the cradle, moving his little hands and legs about, was fixed on EMS's framed portrait hung on the wall. EMS wearing a white shirt and spectacles. Carefully combed, fine, black hair. A bright red background above his head and on either side. The lower half of the picture was awash in the whiteness of the shirt. EMS's shoulders were extraordinarily broad. The portrait had been painted by some local artist. At the bottom right corner of the picture, the long scrawl of the artist's signature could be seen, despite which his name could not be deciphered. Only two letters, 'K' and 'S' were clear.

It was the redness of that picture that attracted Appukkuttan, lying in the cradle. Appukkuttan grew up lying in the cradle and watching that redness.

Having written this much, Kesavan laid the pen down on the table without screwing the cap back on, walked over to the bed and lay down. He fell asleep as soon as he flopped onto the bed.

An autorickshaw came to a halt in the lane. Some people walked up and entered the courtyard, talking loudly.

'It's Ravunni Master and his friends!'

The smell of damp hair struck his face as Sujatha passed close by. She opened the front door. All of them entered the shaded veranda noisily.

'What's the world-class writer doing?' As usual, a shoulder bag was slung across Ravunni's chest. Pavithran and Unni Kurup were with him. All three were sweating profusely.

Securing the mundu firmly around his waist, and pulling on his shirt, Kesavan came down to the verandah.

'We are on our way back to Kozhikode after attending the camp at Kasargode. We thought we'd drop in here.' Ravunni lay back in the easy chair. 'Why didn't you come for the camp?'

'Oh, nothing.' Kesavan said sleepily.

Ravunni moved the bag on his lap down to the floor. His bag was fat and bulging, just like him. He had stuffed all sorts of things into it. His students would always say 'Ravunni Master's bag is always nine months pregnant,' when he was out of earshot.

Kesavan sat staring into the distance, with the melancholy of a truncated afternoon nap lingering on his face.

'Electricity's back,' announced Sujatha. 'You can sit under the fan now.'

'Sujatha, you have put on weight.'

'I realised as much,'she laughed, 'when I couldn't remove the bangles from my wrist!'

Everyone sat under the fan, seeking refuge from the stifling heat. Children returning from schools passed though the lane chattering noisily. Although the silence of the noon had come to an end, Kesavan's silence continued. And although the three of them were his buddies, Kesavan was not without some resentment at their unannounced incursion into his home at this time of the day.

'What are you writing nowadays?' enquired Ravunni.

'Nothing.'

'We heard that you are working on your new novel.'

Kesavan didn't utter a word.

'What's the stuff?'

'Just started...'

'Bring it here. Let me have a look.'

'Ayyo—'

'Bring it, I say!'

Kesavan did not like to show others what he was writing. He believed that till it came out smeared with the printer's ink, what he wrote was his private possession. But Ravunni was stubborn. His friends often likened him to a leech. Wouldn't let go once he bit. Although Pavithran and Unni Kurup were just as eager to read what Kesavan was writing, they kept quiet.

Kesavan stood harried, novel in hand, like a student who had been ordered to stand on the bench for getting his sums wrong.

'Since when have you begun to write using red ink?' Pavithran and Unni Kurup enquired. One ran a tutorial college and the other taught there.

It was for the first time that Kesavan was writing using red ink. He had had to take a bus to the town for buying red ink, since it hadn't been available at the stationery shop in the

Junction. Kesavan didn't respond to Pavithran and Unni Kurup. Unusually, his friends' talk made him uneasy. He wished to be alone at that moment.

'His new novel is about Eeyyemmess,' announced Pavithran, as if only he knew this secret that nobody else was privy to. This was a revelation for Ravunni. The harried expression found earlier on Kesavan's face now migrated to Ravunni's.

'Is it true, Kesavan?'

'Hmmm…'

'What do you know about Eeyyemmess? One shouldn't write about what one doesn't know,' said Ravunni. 'I'd like to remind you about what Vaclav Havel said in the book *Living in Truth*: 'In all my writings, my starting point has always been what I know...''

Kesavan sat there without uttering a word.

'Writers like you, who have always turned their backs on life can't understand Eeyyemmess. He is part of a mass psyche!'

'What! Will you give me a fatwa like the one they gave Salman Rushdie? Will you put a price on my head?'

'Be careful: that is the only thing I have to tell you.'

'No need for any argument now. He has only just begun the novel.' Intervened Unni Kurup.

'I am not arguing with anyone.' Ravunni's tone softened.

'Now, Kesavan, read aloud....' Pavithran leaned forward.

'His father called him Appu. His mother called him Kuttan. And the people... Appukkuttan. Thus, it is the people who made him complete...'

'The beginning is good,' said Pavithran. 'At least now you have accepted the truth that it is the society that gives a fuller existence to the fragmented selves of individuals. So far, so good.'

Ravunni scratched his cheek, and listened intently. Kesavan continued reluctantly:

'Appukkuttan's gaze, while lying in the cradle and moving his little hands and legs about, was fixed on EMS's framed portrait hung on the wall…'

'Read louder, Kesavan...' Though not past thirty, Unni Kurup was hard of hearing. Kesavan continued, raising his voice a little:

> *'… despite which his name could not be deciphered. Only two letters 'K' and 'S' were clear.'*

'Have you read Roland Barthes' *Reality Effect*?' asked Ravunni. 'You need to teach yourself a little more about the art of narration. In *Reality Effect*, Barthes analyses a text by Flaubert. If you had read that, you would not have written in such detail about the long scrawl of the signature of the unknown artist. What is the relevance of the signature of the artist, when you discuss the portrait of an epoch-making personality like Eeyyemmess?'

Kesavan didn't reply.

'There are signs that this novel is going to be very un-Kesavan-like, from the very beginning,'opined Pavithran.

As the reading and discussion continued, Sujatha appeared at the doorway.

'Don't you want tea?'

'No, only a couple of glasses.'

Ravunni fished out a bottle from his fat bag, like a midwife taking out a baby from a pregnant woman's womb.

'Do you have soda?'

'Ayyo, no...'

'Never mind. There's soda in my bag.'

Ravunni took out two bottles of soda as well. He was clearly well-prepared. Maybe there would also be some spicy snack-mixture in his bag.

As the three guests made merry drinking brandy, Kesavan looked on, without drinking anything. 'Hey, you write terrific stories and novels without drinking a drop. If only you drank now and then and wrote...then you would really have become a world-class writer...' Ravunni would often say. Kesavan did not drink. But all his good friends were great boozers. Brandy and arrack turn even grown-ups into children. Look at this Ravunni. When not drunk, he is pig-headed on ideological matters. Two pegs up his gills, he has no hang-ups, no complaints. When not drunk, Ravunni derisively calls Kesavan a 'world-class writer'. But after a couple of drinks, he believes that Kesavan is truly world-class.

'Who used the term 'intertextuality' for the first time?' asked Unni Kurup, like a quiz master, glass of brandy in hand. Without waiting for an answer, he himself added, 'Julia Kristeva.'

When the bottle was empty, silence spread. Sunlight had faded and the trees had darkened. Sujatha served rice for everyone. Ravunni ate, scattering food all over the table and the floor. Satheesan, too, ate in the same way.

Kesavan accompanied them to the gate.

'Wish you and Eeyyemmess all the best!' Ravunni walked down the lane, swinging his now-empty shoulder bag. Unni

Kurup and Pavithran followed. They had to go only till the Fifth Railway Gate by bus, where their tutorial college was located. Teaching and sleeping—they do everything there.

'What is 'intertextuality,' Kesavetta?'

'I'll show you right now. Just come to bed,' he replied. With a twinkle in his eyes, as usual. Though sober, his head felt heavy. So he tumbled into bed early. Thus, one more day in his writerly life had passed, with nothing happening...

Two

Ayyo, Appukkuttan is weeping.

He lies in the cradle, and cries as if the tender muscles in his face and chest would grow taut and snap. But he doesn't shed even a single tear. His is a kind of dry weeping, without tears. How can such a tiny baby cry so loudly? Isn't there a saying, 'small is beautiful'? Why can't one say 'small is powerful' as well? Why not, indeed?

'My God, what's happened to my Kuttan?' Appukkuttan's mother, Sreedevi, was worried. It wasn't like him to cry for nothing. He would wail only when he was hungry. Once his tummy was filled with milk, he would lie moving his little hands and legs about, playing by himself. No one would even know that a baby was lying in the cradle. That was Appukkuttan. One who did not bother anyone.

Look at the neighbour Santha's baby. It sleeps throughout the day and stays up all night. Screaming and raising a din, he never allows anyone to sleep a wink. Appukkuttan wasn't up to any such mischief that turned night into day. He was a meek kid.

Now, what's happened to my Kuttan?

Scooping him up from the cradle and holding him close to her breast, Sreedevi paced the room. After a while, the sound of wailing ceased gradually. Like the steam of the pressure cooker that gushes out and trails off. ('Santha and Vanaja have bought pressure cookers. Only we...' 'We'll also buy one, my dear. As long as I, this Ananthakrishnan, remain alive, all that you want will be bought. Not just a pressure cooker, but a pressure mixie, a pressure washing machine and so on....' 'Don't pull my leg. I am not destined to possess all these....' 'Is it a pressure cooker that decides our destiny?' 'What is the meaning of 'destiny'?' 'An elephant's egg! I ought to carry a dictionary while talking to you.') However, do not think that Appukkuttan's weeping had stopped. Only, he had changed the idiom of his weeping. Now it had turned into sobbing without making the slightest sound. Unusually, torrents of tears rolled down from his eyes. Seeing that tear-streaked silent weeping, Sreedevi's heart ached. Isn't she his mother, who bore him suffering birth pangs? She unhooked her blouse and thrust the nipple of her breast into his mouth. But he turned his face away and continued sobbing.

'Aren't you my darling little son? Drink Amma's milk,' she cajoled him.

Appukkuttan's lips, like a fish's, softly grazed the nipple oozing milk. She looked at his face intently, as if to gauge what was on his mind. A mother can see many things a father cannot possibly detect. But however much she tried, she was not able to divine what was on the child's mind.

Looking at the milk mingled with tears streaking down the corner of his mouth, she continued pacing the room, running her fingers over his hair, smooth as silk.

'My darling Kuttan, please sleep quickly. Do you know how much more work remains to be done? Haven't washed the clothes. Haven't done the grinding. Your father will come in for lunch any time now. What'll I give him then? Sleep, my son...'

As if in answer to her prayers, Appukkuttan's eyes closed slowly. She lowered the open end of the blouse, covering her breast. Only after making sure that he was fast asleep did she lay him back in the cradle. Taking special care not to wake him, she wiped off the milk that streaked down the side of his mouth. If she didn't do that, flies would alight there, zooming in on the faintest trace of milk. Then she tiptoed to the bathroom, to avoid making any noise. There, she had left the clothes soaked, waiting to be washed.

She hadn't reached the bathroom when Appukkuttan's wail rose behind her. He was crying again, piercingly.

'O my Kuttan, I am fed up with you!'

Appukkuttan was weeping, his muscles taut. He shut his eyes tight, as if to prevent from seeing himself cry.

Hearing the scream that came crashing down like the monsoon rains, or rather, a landslide, Santha, the neighbour, came in. 'Give him a little Gripewater. Maybe there are worms inside his tummy.'

'For the last two days I have been telling his father to buy a bottle of Gripewater. He always forgets.'

'Never mind. I'll send Aravindan to buy it.'

Aravindan arrived. He took the money and left.

Neither his family nor the public benefit from Aravindan in any way, as he sat at home without a job after completing his studies.

'Hey you! Where are you going at this high noon?'

It's Moosath who came up to him.

'To buy some Gripewater.'

'What water is that?'

'It's a medicine which cures the worm attack in an infant's stomach.'

'Will it cure the worms in a grown-up's stomach too?'

'I don't know.'

'You don't know a damn thing!'

Moosath went on his way down the lane, using his greying umbrella as a walking stick. His 'Hey you!' had begun only very recently. How else does one address an unemployed loafer!

Must organise some job as soon as possible. And go to office wearing a pair of trousers and a ballpoint pen clipped to the shirt pocket. If not, the next time round, Moosath will say 'Hey, you dog! Where are you going at this high noon?' Not only Moosath, but everyone else as well.

When Aravindan returned with the Gripewater, Sreedevi and Santha were sitting in the verandah. Appukkuttan, limp from crying, lay across Sreedevi's breast. Santha was cleaning the rice of grit and stones, sitting close by.

Sreedevi prised open Appukkuttan's lips and poured in a spoonful of Gripewater.

'Now Appukkuttan will not cry any more,' said Santha. 'It's really terrible if babies get a tummy-ache. What can they do but cry? They can't speak, can they? Whom can they relate their woe to...?'

Santha, who has been through three childbirths, is more knowledgeable about these things than Sreedevi.

Making sure once again that Kuttan was sound asleep, Sreedevi laid him in the cradle. Before she could take her hands off him, he began to bawl again...

When Ananthakrishnan came home for lunch, the oven had not even been lit. Sreedevi was lying face down on the cot. Appukkuttan was sobbing away in the cradle. He was exhausted from the non-stop weeping.

'What happened, Sreedevi?' Ananthakrishnan asked her, in trepidation.

'I wish to die...'

When he saw her face, he knew that she had been crying as well. He went over to the cradle. Seeing his father, Appukkuttan screamed aloud, mustering together all his remaining energy. He had grown enough to recognise his father.

'Who reversed the position of the cradle?' Ananthakrishnan placed the cradle as before, facing the picture of EMS on the wall. Appukkuttan's little eyes raced towards that red picture. And his wailing stopped instantly.

After that he didn't cry at all. Looking at EMS's picture, he played by himself, moving his little arms and legs about...

Stopping there, Kesavan straightened up. When he wrote for a long time sitting in that posture, he developed a backache. Rising, he paced the room, taking one or two rounds. Gripewater for infants when they have a tummy-ache. What kind of water for writers when they have a backache?

'The real water,' as Ravunni might say, 'with a little soda.'

Back in the chair, Kesavan continued writing:

Whenever the son cried, the mother would take EMS's picture and put it near the cradle. Ananthakrishnan's elder brother Ramakrishnan had bought that picture from Andaloorkavu during one of the annual festival fairs. Ananthakrishnan had attempted several times in the past to remove the picture. And had argued and quarrelled with his brother over the matter. Ramakrishnan, who was Ananthakrishnan's senior by over twenty years, had passed away only recently....

Appukkuttan would lie moving his little arms and legs, looking at EMS's picture. He would talk in his own language to EMS and laugh. As long as he could see EMS, he felt no hunger, no thirst.

'We must buy another photo of EMS, and hang it on the wall. A bigger, redder photo,' said Sreedevi. Ananthakrishnan glared at her.

Thus, Appukkuttan grew up.

'Thus, you grew up,' Kesavan rose from the chair. 'From now on, either you grow up or you don't. I don't care. I can't write anymore. Let me lie down a bit.'

Sujatha was grating coconut. The pressure cooker began whistling on the gas stove. The 'weight' atop the cooker began to quiver and swivel. She emptied the grated coconut into the jar of the mixer. When the deafening racket of the mixer rose, together with the whistling of the pressure cooker, he could take it no longer.

He thought wistfully of the times when firewood burned in the oven and rice was cooked in the pot noiselessly. Those were the days....

'I'll be back in a jiffy.' He said, above the din of the mixer.

'Where to?'

'To the Junction.'

'It is the third time you're going to the Junction since this morning. Whom do you want to see? Some of your female fans waiting for the bus?'

'Just for a paan.'

'Long ago, seeing M.T. Vasudevan Nair smoking beedis, boys at college took after him.' Unni Kurup had said. 'And similarly, will college kids also start chewing paan, aping Kesavan?'

'Fat chance!' said Pavithran. 'College kids chewing paan? They want only Pepsi.'

Kesavan got out, putting on a shirt over his sleeveless vest. The damp scent of last night's rain was clinging onto the green patch on the embankment. Little puddles of water lay in narrow crevices on the clay surface of the lane. Rain clouds hung low in the sky.

'Kesavan, wait!' Moosath came up from behind.

'What's it?'

'What are you writing now?'

'Nothing.'

'What did you write about me? Did you describe me as one who always goes up and down the lane?'

'Who said so?'

'You don't need to know that. Did you write that I am too tall and that Visalakshi Ezhuthamma reaches only up to my waist?'

'Who told you all this?'

'I'll come to know whatever you write or say, Kesavan,' said Moosath. 'Write whatever you like about me. Only, you shouldn't write anything about Ezhuthamma.'

Moosath is a minor character in Kesavan's new novel. Not only Moosath, but many others as well.

Moosath's grandson is a student in the tutorial college at the Fifth Railway Gate. The information must have been leaked out by Unni Kurup or Pavithran.

Kesavan and Moosath walked through the lane, chatting and laughing. Moosath deftly jumped over the cowdung that he saw in front of him. Since the cow had dropped the dung just then, a steamy vapour arose from it.

'Kesavetta...!'

Aravindan was standing on the embankment, chewing on the midrib of a coconut leaf for want of something better to do. Though he is very lean, he is broad-shouldered. Shoulders that bear the weight of the future.

Aravindan, too, is a minor character in Kesavan's new novel.

'Kesavetta....'

'What is it?'

'If only you could take a little interest in my case...since you have so many high level contacts....'

'What? Do you take me for a mobile employment exchange? Isn't there a government in place, voted to power by you, your father and the like? Go and ask them to give you a job.' Kesavan was irritated.

'Still, if only you took a little interest...'

'Look here, Aravindan. There is a telephone connection even in this Moosath's Matham. Is there one in my house? Say the word, and the phone will be there. But I won't. That's me. Don't ask me to break that rule for you.'

Aravindan didn't say anything further.

Kesavan and Moosath continued to walk. Traces of fresh dung stuck to the rear of the cow standing near the mud-wall. The cow belonged to Kannan, the owner of the tea shop at the Junction.

'Isn't your leave over?'

'Two more days to go.'

'Why do you have to work in the office? You need only to make a film out of one of your novels.' Nanootti habitually read all the magazines that he hung in his paan shop.

The number of times he chewed paan had increased since he had begun sitting at home on leave, mused Kesavan. As had the chewing of tobacco.

Nanootti spread lime on the betel leaves, added minced betel nut and tobacco, rolled it up and gave it to Kesavan.

The petty shop owners at the Junction are proud that Kesavan comes there, talks and mingles with them. They often see his name and photograph appear in newspapers. Cars and autorickshaws stop at the Junction and invariably ask for directions to reach Kesavan's house. Their locality, hitherto unknown to the outside world, is slowly becoming well-known.

Before evening, he came over to the Junction once again, entered Ponnan's Hair-cutting Saloon and had a fine haircut. Massaging gingelly oil all over his body, he took a hot bath. He lingered over the worship of his body, and the fondling and caressing of each limb. Even as he ate the warm kanji and green gram curry that his wife ladled out, he began to feel drowsy.

His leave ended on Monday. It was with a lot of zest that he woke up that day. He hadn't written anything. Hadn't done anything at all. And his leave was over. Yet, as he prepared to return to office, he felt very happy.

As he was leaving for office, wearing a starched and ironed mundu and shirt and carrying his umbrella and lunchbox, he said to his wife, standing in the verandah:

'I am not one cut out to be a writer. I am just a sarkari babu.'

Three

Kesavan's colleagues welcomed him warmly as he returned to work. A senior colleague even offered to clean his table, and put his papers and other things in order. Amidst the files that were bound in red tape, cigarette and beedi stubs were found heaped up in the lid of a Horlicks jar. In Kesavan's absence, the others must have sat around there in a mood of recreation and smoked. Someone or the other in the office invariably sat on a seat found vacant. Wasn't it boring to sit in one seat continuously and work?

'We never guessed that you'd turn up today.' Lakshmanan from Pannankara spoke in the unmistakable north Malabar dialect. 'Don't you have eight more 'sick leaves' due? You could have come after a few more days.'

'Why should he take leave unnecessarily? It's always reassuring to have some leave in one's credit. Gives one a sense of security. Isn't that so, Kesavan?'

Putting the lunch box on the table that Lakshmanan had cleared, and propping the umbrella against the wall in the corner, Kesavan sat down in his chair. Its backrest, woven with plastic wicker, had become discoloured, due to constant contact with hair oil. The chair had a problem. At times, it would suddenly tilt to one side without warning. Kesavan quipped that his chair was arthritic. The trouble was with its joints. Let it tilt either to the left or to the right. Hasn't any kind of tilt become irrelevant after the advent of perestroika and glasnost? Isn't Mikhail Gorbachev proving that both the left and the right are the same? Kesavan mused, laughing to himself.

'How far has the novel reached, friend?'

'I am still at it.'

'About to finish?'

'Just started.'

'We thought you'd come back only after finishing the novel.'

Kesavan didn't say anything.

'What's the title?'

'*The Novel Unwritten*, okay?' responded Kesavan, with a bitter aftertaste that surged up from within. He felt as if there were many undigested things in his stomach. *Appukkuttan's Lamentations* was the title he had in mind for the new novel. He had made up that misleading statement for his colleagues on purpose.

'A smart title,' opined Lakshmanan.

The title *Novel Unwritten* was an instant hit with his colleagues. Gradually, Kesavan, too, began to like it. Not because of the cuteness of the title, but he literally didn't have to write the novel! He rejoiced at being relieved of the burden of writing the novel. He often dreamt about a life of not writing a single line! Wasn't an ordinary life, that consisted of going to office, helping his wife in the kitchen, helping his son with his math homework and eating and sleeping, good enough for him? Why had he chosen the bothersome vocation of a writer? Bother, nuisance, disturbance, disquiet—he wanted none of this and wished to live the life of the most ordinary citizen, free from all such afflictions. He was afraid of life on a grand scale.

Two years passed. *Appukkuttan's Lamentations* remained an unwritten novel. Kesavan was seriously considering beginning a new one.

'I told you then and there that Eeyyemmess is a theme that would not be handy for you. You should bite off only what you can chew. Haven't you thrown away two full years?'

Kesavan didn't say anything. Ravunni went on: 'I'll do one thing. I suggest that you go on a trip to China. I'll arrange that. It will inspire you.'

'Must I go to China in order to write about Eeyyemmess?'

'You are such a blockhead, literally! However others try to make you understand things, nothing will enter your head.'

'I'm not going anywhere. Whoever wants to meet me can come here.'

Ravunni wasn't pleased by what Kesavan said. His face darkened.

Ravunni has visited Russia and China many times. For him, these countries are like his native Koyilandi.

'I'm off,' he said. 'Got a few bucks?'

Without waiting for a reply, Ravunni plunged his hand into Kesavan's pocket and picked up whatever he found between his fingers, and left. His shoulder bag swang on his arm. Once his bag became empty, he wouldn't hesitate to plunge his hand into someone else's pocket. And he would put forth the justification that money should never idle away in the folds of one's waistband or pocket, and that, on the other hand, it must change hands frequently in its onward journey. The tilt of his money was neither to the left, nor to the right. It was always towards the liquor shop.

It was after the Leftist Government came to power that Ravunni, who used to make do with country arrack earlier, had changed over to brandy. If it was not for the arrack and brandy, he could certainly have become the president of some state-run academy or the chairman of one of those government-owned corporations.

That night when their son was asleep...

'What is it Kesavetta...? If you don't like doing it...'

He lay still. He did not notice the spasms through her thighs beneath his body. Sujatha said something else. Without paying her any attention, he slid off the bed, secured the mundu around his waist and walked towards the writing room.

Lights came on. He retrieved the papers he had written and put away two years ago. He picked up his pen and began writing:

> *Now when Appukkuttan cries, his mother doesn't give him Gripewater anymore. She would, instead, take Eeyyemmess's picture from the wall and put it in the cradle.*
>
> *Appukkuttan grew up conversing, in a language known only to himself, with Eeyyemmess, laughing and playing with him....*

The light shone in Kesavan's writing room until dawn.

Four

'Kuttan's hair has grown like a weed. Must take him to the barber and give him a proper haircut.'

'I'll crop Appu's hair myself,' said Ananthakrishnan. 'Why should we take the kid to the barber at such a tender age?'

Appukkuttan is not yet two. The mother is keenly watching him grow. She is understandably impatient. She is looking forward to seeing Appukkuttan going to school, wearing starched and ironed shorts and shirt, carrying a satchel.

'No. If you cropped his hair, it would look like a crow had pecked his hair off...'

'Hey! I can crop hair much better than the barber Kunhaman can. Do you want to see?'

'Are you capable of doing anything at all? Aren't you the one who shat in your pants encountering the police, in your so-called attempt at ushering in the revolution?' laughed Sreedevi. Ananthakrishnan's face clouded over. This is a ruse she adopts to defeat him in any quarrel. A Naxalite who fled in fright on seeing the police! Just call him that, and he will shut up. Utterly subdued, he will retreat quietly to some corner.

'Ayyo! Are you mad at me? I said that just for the heck of it, Kuttan's father. I'm sorry.'

'I am not angry with anyone. It was after leaving behind all my anger and passion at Pulpalli that I tied the taali around your neck.'

'Didn't I say I was just joking?'

'Take what I said as a joke too.'

'Then pick up Kuttan and go to the barber.'

'It's a pity that you don't let me sit quietly somewhere on a Sunday, Sreedevi.'

'In that case, I'll go myself with the child.'

She knows it doesn't look nice to send a woman to the barber's shop. She also knows that Ananthakrishnan won't permit her to go.

He succumbed to Sreedevi's pressure.

She changed Appukkuttan's dress, powdered his face, marked a black spot on his cheek to ward off the evil eye and handed him over to his father. Appukkuttan played about within the fold of his father's arms. The moment his clothes are changed, he knows that he is going on an outing. Like his mother, he loves to go out, all decked up. Ananthakrishnan's temperament is just the opposite. He doesn't like going out, and prefers to laze around in the house whenever he gets the chance. Or lie down on the cot by the window, enjoying the breeze. That room is the airiest in the house. That's why he moved into that room after his elder brother Ramakrishnan died. It had been Ramakrishnan's room.

The others took away Ramakrishnan's gold ring with the intertwined snakeheads, the gold buttons of his shirt and his gold ear-studs. He had been a bachelor.

'All of you can take away everything. I need only this room.'

The room in which his brother died.

'Hey Appu, be quiet!' Ananthakrishnan admonished Appu, who was squirming in his arms. Appukkuttan was raring to go. As soon as he was dressed up and powdered, he became restless. Once on the road, he would soon become calm and well-behaved. Nestled in his father's arms, he would look at the world with wide-open eyes. He would look at the shops by the wayside, the children waiting at the bus stop, the passing cars, buses and all, with wonder. The world for him was one big spectacle.

Ananthakrishnan walked along the road, carrying Appukkuttan. Wetness lingered on the tarred road from that morning's rain. Petrol, that had leaked from some passing vehicle lay spreading its peacock hues in the wetness.

'Where are father and son headed?' Koren came up and asked by way of bonhomie, a pointed paara for husking coconut slung across his shoulder. He was on his way to husk coconuts in the copra mill. He got eight rupees for husking one hundred coconuts. Though advanced in age, he still husked at least five hundred coconuts a day. By which time, the memory of the toddy shop would also float into his mind. Then and there, he would pull out the paara from the ground and make a beeline for the toddy shop.

'Why don't you tell me?'

'To Kunhaman's. To give Appu a haircut.'

'Go quickly, then. Isn't today a Sunday? It'll be very crowded.' Although he was almost always drunk, Koren remembered dates and days accurately.

Appukkuttan leaned forward and tried to touch the paara on Koren's shoulder.

'What's it, my little one? Do you want this paara? Long ago, your father, with a paara...'

Ananthakrishnan fixed Koren with a stare. Koren was silenced with that piercing look. Without further comment, he walked towards the copra mill.

Oh, it is too much. Everyone has only this to talk about...

Kunhaman's hair-cutting saloon is at the junction where the road branches off to the market. As it was a Sunday, the road and the bus stop were empty. The school and tutorial college were closed. But Kunhaman's saloon was crowded. People had been waiting long before Ananthakrishnan's arrival. You find this kind of rush only on holidays. During the other days, Kunhaman can be seen either dozing off, sitting idly, or stopping the passers-by at his door, discussing politics. Like all barbers, he is also a communist. There isn't a single barber who is a Congressman as far as Ananthakrishnan knows.

'Shaving or cutting?'

'Just 'cutting' for the time being. Appu isn't old enough to be given a shave.'

Hearing Ananthakrishnan, all those who were sitting on the bench laughed uproariously. They made a little space for him to sit down. With Appukkuttan on his lap, Ananthakrishnan settled down at one end of the bench.

The one who is sitting with his face full of soap-lather, with a towel draped around his body, neck downwards, is the manager of the copra mill, Mr Samy. Ananthakrishnan can see his reflection in the mirror. Kunhaman began shaving his face, after whetting the razor and running it over the leather strap a few times. Appukkuttan sat gaping in his father's lap, watching Samy's face covered with lather.

'What's the child's name?'

Kunhaman tilted Samy's head back with some force, propped his chin up and ran the razor from below his chin and upwards. The lather and hair that had piled up on the blade was transferred in one swift move to the top of his left palm.

'Appukkuttan.'

'You've only one child?'

'Umm.' And then he corrected himself mentally. No. *One-and-a-half. One right here, and the half in Sreedevi's womb.*

'Be quick with your job, barber. We have other urgent business,' said the one who was sitting at the other end of the bench. Ananthakrishnan knows him well. He works at the Co-operative Bank. Go through the lane that passes in front of the thannirpandal, till the paddy fields, and turn left: that's his house. He had begun staying in that rented house only recently. Although he remembered all this, he couldn't recall his name.

All the lather has disappeared from Samy's face. After a shave, his face is the colour of a sloughed snake. Taking off the cloth wound around him neck down, Kunhaman rubs his cheeks hard with a block of alum. Ananthakrishnan didn't know why barbers rubbed the face with that stone after a shave. He didn't want to know anything nowadays. He had even forgotten words such as 'interest' or 'curiosity.'

As Ananthakrishnan was musing with relief that Samy's shave was over, Samy got up and lifted his left hand, revealing a bushy armpit to the barber. Then the right hand. Kunhaman plain-shaved the armpits. Ananthakrishnan could see the bare armpits.

'Next,' said Kunhaman. He knows only one word in English. And that is 'next'.

The one who was sitting at the other end of the bench got up in a hurry and took the seat vacated by Samy.

'Cutting?'

'Both. Don't crop the back of the head using the machine-scissors. Use plain scissors for that,' said Suku Nair. Yes, his name is Suku Nair, Ananthakrishnan suddenly remembered.

Appukkuttan was struggling to slide down from Ananthakrishnan's lap. The red mud floor is covered with cut hair and shorn beards. It is into that mess that Appukkuttan was trying to wriggle down. Ananthakrishnan sat holding him back, pushing him firmly onto his lap.

There were two others who had arrived before him, sitting on that bench. His turn would come only after theirs. Would Appukkuttan sit still that long? He had already begun sobbing. Ananthakrishnan felt resentment welling up inside him against Sreedevi, who had sent him out on such a mission on a holiday.

Seeing his predicament, Kunhaman said: 'You can come next.' Neither person waiting on the bench said a word in protest. They had been watching Appukkuttan's antics as well.

Kunhaman didn't have to work very hard on Suku Nair's head since there wasn't much hair left. On his face too, the hair was scanty. The hunger of the razor that had confronted his facial hair would hardly have been satiated. After the cutting and shaving, Suku Nair's head and face looked almost tin-plated.

'Now the little one's.' Kunhaman stretched out both his hands to pick up Appukkuttan. There were traces of soap lather and cut hair on his forehands. Turning his face away, Appukkuttan clung onto his father's neck.

It is such a taxing affair to cut a little child's hair. It requires a lot of patience. Precisely what Kunhaman lacks.

'My God, let no one come with a child today!' he used to pray during the time he had just set up his hair-cutting saloon.

'Hey Kunhaman! Weren't you too a child once? Barbers would cut your hair too, wouldn't they? What is it? Have you forgotten all that now?' Kunhaman had then heard God admonish him in his sleep.

And thus God would speak to him now and then. God's speech was in the plain Malayalam of north Malabar. He had long suspected that God was a native of Eramala. But when Anthony from Mangalore, who sharpens scissors and razors with the knife sharpener, told him that it was in Konkani that God spoke to him, Kunhaman had been flabbergasted.

Ananthakrishnan sat Appukkuttan in the revolving chair and stood guard nearby. Kunhaman covered Appukkuttan with the same cloth he had used on the copra mill manager Samy and the Co-operative Bank clerk Suku Nair. Appukkuttan squirmed and tried to knock it away. Kunhaman cut one lock of hair with his scissors. Appukkuttan's hair was like silk. Kunhaman felt a kind of ecstasy cutting his hair. Not only Appukkuttan's hair; he yearned to cut everything he set his eyes on. One of Kunhaman's fond wishes was to circumcise a Muslim. However, for that one had to become an Ossan, not a mere barber. He had often considered converting to Islam just to be able to circumcise children. Kunhaman lacked the ability to identify his own black humour. For the same reason, he didn't smile a dark smile, either. Kunhaman isn't one who cracks jokes and laughs on hearing them. Doesn't a passion for violence lurk in the mind of this brooding person? Some Congressmen have sensed this. That's why certain Congressmen, while sitting in the revolving chair with the cloth draped around them below their neck, are filled with consternation to see Kunhaman whet the razor on the leather strap. They have begun to recognise the fact that an exclusive haircutting saloon for Congressmen is indeed necessary in that area. But so far they have not been able to find a single barber who is pro-Congress. If all barbers are communists, how can poor Congressmen sit inside a saloon and have their hair cut and face shaven with any sense of security?

'Hey Kunhaman, you are indeed lucky,' Gopalan Master, who kicked the bucket getting drunk all the time, had said while holding forth on some subject. 'How many people's heads you are able to actually hold in your hand!'

Yes, so many heads...heads of all shapes and sizes. Heads that think so many different thoughts. Grieving heads. Dreaming heads. Angry heads...

Appukkuttan, who was sitting, covered all over, with his tiny legs folded in the chair, suddenly leapt up. The scissors flew out of Kunhaman's hands.

'Eeyyemmech!' Appukkuttan pointed his tiny finger at the mirror.

Ananthakrishnan, who was bending forward, looked at the mirror. From the depths of the mirror, the bespectacled Eeyyemmess smiled back at him. Straightening up and turning around, he looked at the wall behind. Above the heads of those who sat waiting their turn, a small framed photo of Eeyyemmess hung on the wall. It had not caught his attention so far.

Five

Tragedy Number One:

Ananthakrishnan, fair and stockily built, is only five feet two inches tall. A person of that height need not necessarily be called a dwarf. It is because of his bulk that Ananthakrishnan appears short. If he were not so fat, he would merely look small-made and no one could have called him a dwarf. Nobody pokes fun at small-built men. Weren't Napoleon Bonaparte and Charlie Chaplin men of short stature? They were never derided for that, were they?

'You could trust a thief, but never a dwarf,' Ananthakrishnan heard the Two Drunks sitting on the culvert quote as he passed by. His heart gave a violent lurch. Didn't that imply that he was worse than a thief? Weren't they stone drunk and out of their wits; forget about it, he told himself. But he couldn't forget it in a hurry. Only that the drunks had blurted out openly what many others were saying privately. Ananthakrishnan believes that a drunken man never lies.

As time passed, Ananthakrishnan's hairline receded. When he combed his hair, strands of hair would fall from the teeth of the comb. Baldness attacked him quite suddenly. The area just above his forehead soon became a wasteland.

'There is no remedy for baldness and envy,' the Two Drunks sitting on the culvert quoted another adage.

I am a dwarf, worse than a thief, he said to himself. And an envious baldie, to boot.

'Here's twenty rupees.'

'What for, saar?'

'Go, have two shots of arrack.'

'Ayyo, saar...'

'Not a word more. Take this money.'

They took the money reluctantly.

'You must speak the truth always, as you did now. You must speak aloud, looking in one's face, what others say in secret.'

The Two Drunks stood with palms joined in reverence, uncomprehending.

Their names were Ittaman and Idi Peter respectively. Although Ittaman is a headload worker, he does not belong to the Centre of Indian Trade Unions, (CITU) the Marxist Party trade union. It is because of his excessive drinking that the door of CITU doesn't open for him. Ananthakrishnan doesn't know what Peter's trade is. The name of Idi Peter—or 'Punch Peter'—fell to his lot not because he punched others, but because he regularly got *punched by others.*

The truth the Two Drunks had declared remained in Ananthakrishnan's heart like a raw wound.

'We shouldn't have said that,' said the First Drunk when Ananthakrishnan was out of earshot.

'It's not we who said that. It's God who made us say that,' said the Second Drunk.

'The poor fellow's heart must have smarted. A pity.'

'Is his heart that easily hurt? He is a Naxalite.'

'Would a Naxalite go to a temple or a church?'

'Did you see him go to a temple?'

'I did.'

Who doesn't know that Ananthakrishnan is a devotee of Mathappura Muttappan and Subramanya Swamy of Palani? While the Two Drunks were sitting in the arrack shop with the money Ananthakrishnan gave them, the latter was standing, palms folded, in front of the picture of the Palani Swamy who has the peacock as his mount.

As early as his schooldays, the signs of a heterodox had been discernible in Ananthakrishnan. It was by questioning established beliefs and superstitions that Ananthakrishnan had caught the attention of his own family.

Just as in every other household, Ananthakrishnan's family too followed the practice of lighting the traditional oil lamp in the front verandah in the evening, after which the children, sitting in its circle of light, would chant the name of God.

'Coconut oil is so scorchingly expensive. Why waste it so, burning the lamp, Chechi?'

Holding the seven-wicked nilavilakku in her hand, the elder sister stared at her little brother in dismay.

'What nonsense are you talking, Ananthakrishnan?'

'Chechi, we need a lamp only in darkness. Here, it is well-lit.'

'Who gives you all these notions? Haven't I told you time and again not to mingle with the communists?'

Chechi bent low, set the lamp down on the cowdung-coated verandah and straightened up; then, closing her eyes and praying silently, she returned to the interior of the house, rubbing her oil-smeared fingertips on her hair.

'Ayyo, Chechi, Ananthakrishnettan blew out the lamp!' shouted the children' who had been chanting God's name. Hearing the commotion, Chechi returned. Smoke was rising from the wicks of which the flames had been extinguished. The smell of burnt coconut oil wafted in the air.

'Ananthakrishnan, your arrogance is exceeding all limits!'

It was then that Ramakrishnan walked into the house, returning home on foot from the office, two-and-a-half miles away, panting and puffing from the brisk walk. His feet and the tip of his furled umbrella, which he used as a walking stick, were covered in slush. Climbing on to the verandah and hanging the umbrella on the eaves, Ramakrishnan looked at everyone, his gaze shifting from one face to another, over and over again.

'Ananthakrishnettan blew out the lamp,' reported the children. 'How are we to chant God's name, now?'

'Good he did that,' said Ramakrishnan. 'Coconut oil is scorchingly expensive.'

The children, who had stopped the chanting, ran hither and thither in mirth. Without uttering a word, Chechi went inside and sat there weeping.

The First Drunk: 'Shall we polish off another shot?'

The Second Drunk: 'Yes, let's.'

One shot each of arrack dropped into their glasses with broken rims.

The First Drunk: 'Hey Idi Peter, you know, when Ananthakrishnan was studying in college the police used to raid his house frequently. That's when he went underground.'

The Second Drunk: 'That's how he became a Naxalite. Isn't it so, Ittaman?'

The Two Drunks, even as they drank arrack with his money, continued to discuss Ananthakrishnan. In the meanwhile, they shouted at the bearer saying that the arrack didn't have enough tang and tasted like sherbet. And demanded two green chillies, which they chewed and swallowed along with the arrack.

'Because of Ananthakrishnan it has become impossible to go out. How can we face people? Such things never happened in this family,' his mother said in consternation. 'Whom can I talk to about my grief? The one I could talk to has deserted me, gone ahead of me.' The mother looked heavenward.

Mother and daughter had formed one bloc. And Ramakrishnan and Ananthakrishnan, the other one.

Ananthakrishnan pelted stones at buses, set a police station ablaze and consequently went to jail. He knocked down the sentry with a paara, staged a jail-break and went underground. Meanwhile, the police caught Ramakrishnan, who had committed no crime, and put him behind bars.

The First Drunk: 'His mother and elder sister swallowed the fire of anxiety.'

The Second Drunk: 'Wasn't he playing with fire?'

The First Drunk: 'Though he knocked down the policeman with a paara, he is compassionate. How else could he have given us twenty rupees for our shots of arrack?'

The Second Drunk: 'If only he had given us thirty rupees, we could have had a couple of shots more.'

The Two Drunks stumbled out of the arrack shop, belching loudly. Arrack and green chillies were burning in their bowels.

'We have also swallowed fire!' The Two Drunks laughed, clapping their hands, standing in the street. 'In our bowels too there's fire....'

A few years ago...

'I am sleepy...'Ananthakrishnan said to Saravanan. Both of them had gone underground and were living in the jungle. Saravanan was as thin as a chicken leg. Like Charu Majumdar.

An afternoon. Dusk descends on the jungle early. They could hear the wing beats of flying foxes overhead. The kite-like wing of a flying fox was caught in a tree branch as it flew in. It was struggling to extricate the wing, which had been sundered into two like a piece of cloth.

'I want to enjoy a long sleep.' Ananthakrishnan's drowsy voice was drowned by the racket raised by the flock of flying foxes surrounding the entrapped one.

The coo of turtle doves mingled with the racket. The wild frangipani tree was full of turtle doves. Ever since they came to live in hiding in Ankakkavu, they had lived mostly on roasted dove-meat. Ankakkavu, a sacred grove devoid of rituals like the lighting of the lamp and the Vellattu performance for dead ancestors, was a place where people did not venture. Although there was a deity, no one came to offer worship. Even those who come tending goats would not come anywhere near the kavu. This proved to be a blessing for the outlaws.

'Now, where is the time to sleep?'

'I can't help laying my head down a bit.'

'Why are you talking as if you are not in your right senses, Ananthakrishnan? This is not your home. It's the jungle. And we are in hiding.'

'I know that.'

'And yet, why do you say that you want to sleep?'

'Can I help it if I feel sleepy?'

'Go to that stream and wash your face properly. Or take a dip. Your sleep will flee.'

How many times he had washed his face! How many times he had bathed! Each time he finished a bath, he felt still sleepier.

'There is no time to chat away. Kunhikkannan Master will be arriving shortly. Bundle up whatever you want to take and prepare for the journey. We have a long way to go.'

'Saravanan! It seems that that flying fox is dead.'

'We could have roasted it. But, where is the time now for that?'

'It'd be better if it's dead. Much better than struggling like this on a torn wing.'

'I don't at all like these sentiments of yours, Ananthakrishnan. Flying foxes, doves and all are for us to eat and satisfy our hunger with.'

Subsisting on the meat of doves and flying foxes, Saravanan had put on weight of late. Three meals a day of roast meat!

'Get up, my dear Ananthakrishnan. Don't you know that we have to reach Kallaippara before dark? We mustn't keep Kunhikkannan Master waiting. We should sympathise at least a little with that old man who suffers from backache. We have so much of time ahead of us to sleep to our fill. Just wait for that time.'

Ananthakrishnan didn't stir.

Saravanan brought water in a coconut shell and sprinkled it on Ananthakrishnan's face. Shook him hard. Losing patience, he kicked and poked at him. And even pulled at his hair. And yet, Ananthakrishnan didn't stir from the base of that tree. He glared at Saravanan like a wounded wild boar. Saravanan felt that Ananthakrishnan would attack him if he provoked him any further. He knew that he was not strong enough to counter Ananthakrishnan, whose body was as hard as a rock. Automatically, he took two steps backward.

'You are a class enemy. You are a fifth column. You won't escape the consequences of this. Don't think you can escape from this jungle. Your end will come here! Look, like that flying fox!' Saravanan pointed to the flying fox that hung from the tree branch.

Lying amidst the cooing turtle doves of the kavu, Ananthakrishnan slept till dawn. Neither the cold of the jungle nor the mosquito bites disturbed his sleep. When he opened his eyes, it was daybreak.

In the light that filtered in through the green canopy, he saw a girl carrying a baby in her arms, staring at him. One end of the cord of her skirt was touching her knee. Looking at him, she smiled, bewilderment still lingering on her face.

Ananthakrishnan didn't know whether that girl carrying a child was a dream or for real.

From then on, Ananthakrishnan lived like an ordinary person. He stopped reading. He spent his time playing cards and watching lowbrow movies. Once when he was returning home after a movie's second show, some people waylaid him.

'What do you want, folks?'

'We have come to put you to sleep. From now on, you can sleep comfortably, lying in the cradle.'

'Comrades, sleep is the other side of wakefulness.' The marauders didn't hear him as he said that, lying in a pool of blood on the road.

Ananthakrishnan was grievously injured. As is usual in such attacks, the first blow had been to the head. God has given the human race thick skulls in order to protect communists and ex-communists from assaults and attempted assassinations. Ananthakrishnan's skull was as strong as a tortoise shell. It was solely due to the hardness of his skull that he had been saved. And yet, six stitches had to be administered to his head.

Whenever he looks back at his past, Ananthakrishnan always feels that it would have been far better had he been dead that day. It was not because he was eager to live that he had quit the Movement. It was because he did not have the capacity to kill other people. His mind was not as hard as his skull. If only he had a shell as strong as a tortoise's that could protect the mind like the skull protects the brain.... If he were God, he would put the human mind within a strong casing. The mind, which is easily cut and bruised like the brain, needs security like the brain as well.

The First Drunk: 'Ayyo, my glass is empty.'

The Second Drunk: 'Mine too.'

The Two Drunks got out and began to walk on unsteady legs. For them, the noontime sunshine appeared like midnight moonshine.

Six

Tragedy Number Two:

Now it remained for Kesavan to narrate the second tragedy in Ananthakrishnan's life. The question of how effectively to handle it continued to pose a challenge for him. Because it was a very commonplace event—so commonplace that it did not deserve any space in a novel or even in newspapers or magazines. For him, presenting simple things was really difficult. And portraying complex situations was not problematic at all! No wonder then that Ravunni had commented in one of his recent essays that 'Kesavan's pen specialises in unravelling knotty plots'.

What confuses Kesavan is the conviction that such an ordinary event ought not to occur in Ananthakrishnan's extraordinary life. If Ananthakrishnan had been a headload worker, toddy tapper or a coppersmith, Kesavan would not have faced such a dilemma. For the event was one which blended seamlessly into the life of ordinary people like the aforementioned.

But Ananthakrishnan was no ordinary person. He had been ardently involved in extremist activities and had even gone underground. He had been indicted in several cases where houses and police stations had been set on fire and landlords beheaded. He had come out unscathed only because there was no concrete evidence in some of the cases and he had turned approver in the others. Flinging away his past like a useless chappal, he had bid adieu to the Movement and turned inactive one fine day. And although he had tried to convince both himself and others that he was just an ordinary person like, say, one who soldered old vessels, he could never really become one.

Kesavan required only a few words to portray this change in Ananthakrishnan's life, which the ex-Naxalite leader K. Venu had described as a miserable and destructive transformation within the premises of ideology. Portraying an extremist who had fed on the roasted meat of a turtle dove—the very symbol of peace—Kesavan's pen could effortlessly create an atmosphere of conflict between spirituality and ideology. This portrayal was all the more effective because the turtle dove could be established as a signifier.

However, Kesavan was unable to find such a symbol to portray the second tragedy in Ananthakrishnan's life.

Ananthakrishnan's wife Sreedevi and the infant died in childbirth—this was the second tragedy of Ananthakrishnan's life. The wife of a revolutionary who had been active in armed struggle, and who had brought about a great turnaround in ideological premises, ought not to have courted such a simple and direct death. Her death would have matched Ananthakrishnan's eminence if she had died of some intellectual sort of disease such as Alzheimer's or Parkinson's. I shouldn't have let Ananthakrishnan's wife die in childbirth like some carpenter's or goldsmith's wife, Kesavan said to himself.

This incongruity, which was of his own making, troubled Kesavan.

He attempted to escape the uneasiness by justifying it in the light of a new line of logic.

This was Kesavan's justification:

Ananthakrishnan is not an armed revolutionary anymore. He has left behind politics and philosophy. In such a person's life, the ordinariness of the fact that his wife and baby died in childbirth does not create any incongruity. Because Ananthakrishnan is himself an ordinary person now. Regressing into a trivial, lowly life.

The incongruity that had disturbed Kesavan at once became congruent and he was quite pleased with himself.

But the pleasure didn't last long. Another problem of characterisation loomed large before him.

The new problem:

Kesavan calculated that Sreedevi and baby must have died in the seventies. Hadn't there been hospitals with maternity departments during that period? Weren't facilities for caesarean surgery available then? In an earlier chapter, Kesavan had mentioned that there was a bank in Ananthakrishnan's area. But he did not know whether there was a hospital with a maternity ward and modern facilities as well. Sometimes Kesavan is like God, ignorant about his own creations.

If Sreedevi's death is to be portrayed in a credible manner, first the circumstances leading to it had to be narrated and established. How did Sreedevi lose her life in childbirth? Did she have a serious ailment like hypertension or jaundice? Kesavan doesn't know. The fact is that he hadn't thought about it. If he had recognised the need for introducing a disease to justify

Sreedevi's death, he could easily have solved the problem. In any case, he needed only a few words to give her one: 'As she opened her eyes in the morning with the feebleness induced by fever, she saw the sun yellow as a bell-flower.' With just this sentence, the readers would infer that Sreedevi had been affected by jaundice. And if she died in childbirth shortly after, the readers would take it as quite natural. There was no need to describe to the well-informed Malayalee readership that jaundice is a dangerous disease.

However, Kesavan was not aware of such things. It was only when Sreedevi had breathed her last that he realised that he had not given her any disease to lead up to her death. As a novelist, it was a mistake he had committed in the area of characterisation. The only way out for him now was to add that there wasn't a hospital with facilities for a Caesarean surgery in Ananthakrishnan's locality. Upon second thoughts, Kesavan realised that even that was not going to be effective. Whichever rustic outback Ananthakrishnan hailed from, it was unlikely that there was no hospital with modern facilities at least ten or fifteen kilometres away. It is not in Bihar that Ananthakrishnan lives, but in Kerala, Kesavan said to himself.

Kesavan felt an extreme sense of mortification. He paced up and down his room. Later, he came out onto the verandah and continued walking, as he had found it impossible to move without encountering the obstacles of the writing table, chair, easy chair and the shirt stand in the writing room....

Seven

With Sreedevi's passing away, Ananthakrishnan and Appukkuttan became all alone in the world.

'Doesn't matter. So many people live like this. We too will live on, won't we, Appu?'

He picked up Appukkuttan, who was playing about with kunnikkuru seeds, and held him up above his head. The child laughed, shaking all over. Ananthakrishnan also tried to laugh along with him. But then a bitter taste rose from the pit of his stomach up to his throat. Appukkuttan sat astride his father's shoulder, dangling tiny legs and stroking his bald head. He was very fond of his father's bald head.

It was his mother who used to call him 'Kuttan'. With her passing away, he became merely 'Appu' at home. For the people, however, he was still 'Appukkuttan.' They had a soft corner for the motherless child. As he walked to nursery school holding his father's hand, the shopkeeper would call out:

'Appootta, d'you want an ellunda?'

'Appootta, have a toffee!'

Appukkuttan would shake his head. His mother had taught him not to accept anything that others offered for free. And although

Sreedevi was not around anymore, Appukkuttan obeyed her instructions.

Ananthakrishnan went to work only once in a while. He was on leave most of the time. No one else in his office availed of leave like he did. The neighbours even wondered if he still did have a job at all. While others worked in the office, Ananthakrishnan washed Appukkuttan's bottom, bathed him and fed him. Like Sreedevi, he focused all his attention on Appukkuttan.

Appukkuttan would call out for his mother only when he was hungry. 'Mother, I'm hungry!' he would say. For him, she was to be remembered only when he was hungry. Ananthakrishnan was relieved to note that Appukkuttan was otherwise beginning to forget his mother rather quickly.

Children can easily forget anything.

A year passed.

Once, Appukkuttan was down with a raging fever. He was in the grip of a severe attack of mumps. When he lay there in delirium, he called out: 'Father, Father...!' Ananthakrishnan's happiness knew no bounds on hearing this. From now on, perhaps he would call out to his father when he was hungry too. With that, memories of Sreedevi wouldn't trouble him any longer.

The phlegm in Appukkuttan's chest complicated matters. Appukkuttan coughed and writhed in spasms of suffocation. Throughout the night, Ananthakrishnan paced the room, cradling Appukkuttan in his arms. He was a big child by then. Ananthakrishnan's hands ached under the strain of his weight. And walking up and down, his legs ached as well.

Ananthakrishnan had the lingering suspicion that Sreedevi was trying to snatch away the child from him. She wanted her son. She, who is obviously selfish, doesn't even care about Ananthakrishnan. Who would be left for him, if Appu deserted him too?

No, Sreedevi, no....

Ananthakrishnan admitted Appukkuttan to a hospital in the city. In fact, he had run all the way to the city. People looked on in dismay as Ananthakrishnan raced down the road with the child in his hands, and not a single autorickshaw in sight. He knew that there wouldn't be any bus or autorickshaw available when there was urgent need of one. In desperation, he ran up the slope. Once they crossed the slope, they would reach the market. Surely there would be autorickshaws in the market area...

As he kept vigil beside his son, lying on an iron cot in the hospital, he entreated God to intervention against Sreedevi. He beseeched God not to let her anywhere near that hospital.

That sleepless night, he undertook a major vow. If Appukkuttan recovered, he would ascend the Palani Hill on foot with his son. Subramanya Swamy of Palani was his favourite deity. He had great faith in Subramanya Swamy's power and compassion.

The swelling in his throat, the phlegm in his lungs and the fever gone, Appukkuttan soon became well again and was back home.

'Anantheshna, you were hard put with your son falling sick, weren't you?' said Narayani Chechi' who had come visiting, hearing the news. She was his uncle's eldest daughter. In his childhood, she would wash his bottom when he shat in the open. He remembered that even now. Whenever he went over to Uncle's house, he would insist upon having his bottom washed by Narayani Chechi.

'Couldn't you at least drop a line? I am burdened with my own family and its problems... The arthritis on the leg of the father of my children is worsening day by day. Can't walk even a step. And since

so long, too…Though he can't move his leg, he has produced quite a few children! Do I not have to feed them all and bring them up? This Chechi has time only for that. Anantheshna, my life is truly hell. Still, my dear, why didn't you let me know that you were struggling here? Wouldn't this Chechi have come running?'

'It's all right,' replied Ananthakrishnan.

'Don't say a word more. I know that you can't bring up Appu all by yourself. I have found a girl for you. Don't think up any excuses now. Aren't you just thirty-one? Such a long stretch of life remains ahead of you. How can you spend all this time just by yourself? Don't you have a son to look after? Don't you need someone to cook food and feed him regularly?'

'I am more than enough to cook food and feed him, Chechi.'

'You were always good at repartees...'

'What did you come for, Chechi? To see the unwell Appoottan or get me to marry?'

'Am I an outsider, my dear? Aren't I your Chechi, your elder sister? Can I help swallowing fire thinking about your plight, my son?'

'I will look after my own affairs. No one need swallow fire on account of me and my son. I will swallow it all by myself. Don't you know, Chechi, that I am used to swallowing fire?'

'O my Anantheshna, I don't understand what you are saying. Don't marry if you don't want to. Perhaps it is your fate that you must live alone. But, can't you come over to the ancestral home and stay there with all of us? There are any number of people to look after Appoottan. It's really difficult to understand you, my dear.'

Ananthakrishnan laughed to himself. I cannot understand my own self. How can you, then, understand me?

'I have said whatever I had to say. Now everything is up to you. I'm leaving….'

Chechi opened her umbrella, climbed down the stairs and left. It was only afterwards that he realised that he hadn't offered even a cup of tea to her.

Eight

Father and son, clad in ochre, had set out to beg for alms, with a tin can as a begging bowl. They must finish at least twenty-five houses before the sun was up, Ananthakrishnan decided. It would be difficult to go about doing the ritual begging with Appukkuttan in the scorching sun. He was still off-colour after the attack of mumps. He had not regained his earlier verve and vivaciousness. Appukkuttan was fed milk morning and evening—Bournvita in the morning and Complan at night. And yet, he had not become his old self again. At any rate, he was at least alive! As he watched the tender veins in his son's hands being pierced by the intravenous needle through which glucose would be fed into his bloodstream, Ananthakrishnan had feared that he would never come back to life.

Holding his son's hand, Ananthakrishnan set out to beg before seven in the morning.

'Yyo... we've become Swamy!' shouted Appukkuttan, looking at Ananthakrishnan's ochre mundu. Appukkuttan's clothes were also dyed ochre.

'Where are we going, Father?'

'To Padmavathy's house.'

'Why are we going there?'

'Aren't you telling me all the time that we must go there?'

'Let's not go today, Father. Appoottan's not well today.'

'If we don't go today, Palani Swami will get angry.'

'Let him.'

'Ayyo…' Ananthakrishnan hastily covered Appukkuttan's mouth. 'O Palani Subramanya Swamy! My son has said this, ignorant of the consequences. Please forgive him… My son is so innocent!'

They went to Gopala Kurup's house next door, first. It was a tiled house with a verandah enclosed by iron grille. As they knew in advance about Ananthakrishnan's visit, Gopala Kurup and his wife Saudamini were waiting for them. From the yard, Ananthakrishnan called out 'Swamy!' thrice. Kurup's wife dropped a fistful of rice into the tin can in Ananthakrishnan's outstretched hand. The 'ration' rice stank.

Seeing Appukkuttan standing there without uttering a word, Kurup coaxed him: 'Why don't you call out to Swamy too, my son? It is Palani Swamy who saved you. It is for your sake that your father is taking so much of trouble. Call out 'Swamy' thrice.'

'Appoottan wants to pee,' replied Appukkuttan.

'Pee under that drumstick tree.'

Appukkuttan went over to the drumstick tree, did the job and came back. One leg of his shorts was wet with urine. There was urine on his knee as well.

'You don't even know how to pee without wetting your shorts, yet you have grown so big,' hissed Ananthakrishnan in a whisper. However Saudamini had heard it and began to laugh at him.

When they reached the alley and were climbing down the embankment, Appukkuttan said irritably:

'Appoottan doesn't want to become Swamy. Appoottan wants to go home.'

'It was just for fun that Saudamini Amma laughed so. Take it easy.'

'I want to go home,' he persisted.

How could they? There were a hundred houses to visit and beg alms from. Was Appukkuttan fed up so soon?

Holding his son's hand, he climbed up the embankment once again and reached Aravindan's house. Ananthakrishnan took out a conch-shell from his bag and blew it. And called out aloud 'Swamy' three times. On seeing the conch, Appukkuttan was enthusiastic once more.

'Appootan wants to blow the conch.'

'You won't be able to. Only grown-ups can.'

'Appoottan wants to blow it!'

He threw a tantrum for the conch.

Hearing the blowing of the conch, Aravindan's elder sister Santha came out. She was carrying a baby on her hip. Its lips were moist with Gripewater. It was Santha's third child. As soon as children began crying, Santha would pour Gripewater in their mouths. She made them drink Gripewater regardless of whether her children cried after being bitten by an ant, or because of hunger.

'Give me that bag here, Anantheshnetta,' she said, coming over with a fistful of rice. Receiving the offering in the tin can, he transferred it into the bag. This, too, was ration rice.

'When are you going to Palani?' asked Aravindan, from the far end of the verandah, dangling his legs. Ananthakrishnan had not noticed him sitting there.

'After completing begging in one hundred and one houses.'

'May I too join you?'

'What for?'

'I am tired of begging in front of humans for a job. Now let me turn to the gods. If they can...'

'The gods will certainly heed your cry. Swamy, Swamy...'

Picking up the end of the ochre mundu and holding Appukkuttan's hand, Ananthakrishnan climbed down into the alley. He tried to draw a mental map of the houses he was to visit. Appukkuttan, who was walking along holding his father's hand, had his mind set on the conch in the bag.

'Appoottan wants that conch!'

'Stop talking and walk fast, my son.'

Their next stop was at the house of Kunhiraman Master, the Malayalam teacher in the local school. He had taught Ananthakrishnan Malayalam till class eight. Kunhiraman Master was quite old. Both his legs were full of sores and black as burnt wood below the knees. Master was lying in the easy chair reading a magazine when they visited him. Though old, Master didn't need glasses to read. He had recognised Ananthakrishnan from quite a distance off.

Standing in the courtyard, Ananthakrishnan blew on his conch and called out 'Swamy' three times.

'Well done, Anantheshna. God has retrieved you from the pit of sin. Good that you are giving thanks to God for that.'

'All for my son.'

'Whomever it is for, trust in God is good.'

Ananthakrishnan looked at his teacher's face, world-weary. Kunhiraman Master's wife, Deviyamma, came with rice in her cupped palms. She poured it into the bag Ananthakrishnan held out. It was the Muthichempa variety of rice. When cooked, it would be as fine and white as thumba flowers.

'Keep this too. Isn't it an offering to God?'

Kunhiraman Master put a one rupee coin in Ananthakrishnan's can.

'Let's buy ellunda with that,' suggested Appukkuttan as they walked out of Master's house. 'That's for Palani Swamy, my son,' Ananthakrishnan said.

'We can give the Swamy some ellunda as well.'

'Walk fast without talking. Do you know how many more houses we have to visit today?'

'Whose house are we going to visit now?'

'Now we are...'

'Let's go to Chathu Maestry's. There is a guava tree in their yard. Appoottan wants to eat guava.'

'How do you know?' Ananthakrishnan was at a loss as to when Appukkuttan might have gone over to Chathu Maestry's house.

'That's what Padmavathy said. That there is a guava tree in the backyard of Maestry's house.'

'Now we are going to Koman Vaidyar's.'

They walked towards Koman Vaidyar's house, about two furlongs away. The sight of father and son going about clad in ochre and blowing a conch, was a curious spectacle for the passers-by.

Vaidyar's house was an old two-storey building. At the crack of dawn, the labourers had spread out copra and arecanut in the yard to dry. It was not through practising the Vaidyars' profession as physician that he amassed all his wealth, but by selling copra. He had foreseen that the age of herbs and kashayam had passed, and had sent both his sons to a medical college in Karnataka. Both were doctors of modern medicine now.

'Who's here? Isn't it our Anantheshnan?' Vaidyar's wife, Kuttiyamma, placed her index finger on her nose, in a sign of utter amazement.

'It is Anantheshnan indeed. It's I who treated him and his elder brother Rameshnan when they were children. Both had eczema on their buttocks, off and on.'

Ananthakrishnan and Appukkuttan reached the courtyard.

Kuttiyamma brought rice in a reed-woven muram. She emptied it into the bag.

'Give us money too,' said Appukkuttan.

Hearing that, Koman Vaidyar laughed, revealing broken teeth. He took out a quarter rupee from his waistband and put it in the can.

'Very smart. What's your name?'

'Appoottan.'

'Appootta, haven't you come for begging alms? You should then accept what you receive. You shouldn't be asking for specific things like rice or money.'

Vaidyar reached out to stroke Appukkuttan's head with a hand covered with grey down. As they walked back, Appukkuttan picked up a piece of copra from the yard.

'Father, are we beggars?'

'It's all God's play. You will understand when you grow up.'

'When will I grow up?'

'You should drink milk daily with Bournvita before you go to school. And you should study well. Then you'll grow up fast.'

'Should I drink Complan too?'

Father and son were exhausted by the time they finished fifteen houses. Appukkuttan was perspiring and his feet were covered with mud and grime. Seating his son on his shoulder, slinging the ochre cloth bag around his neck and with conch in hand, Ananthakrishnan walked along the mud-dyke of the paddy fields. His ears were burning in the hot sun.

'You should be ashamed of yourself... Conch in the hand that wielded the gun!'

Ananthakrishnan turned around, startled. He could not see anything other than the expanse of the paddy fields drying up in the sun. Who had said that? Was it a mere day dream?

They finished ninety houses within three days. But then there was a mishap. As they entered the courtyard of the coir factory owner, a dog rushed in barking ferociously. Appukkuttan flushed with fear. This was a real shock for him.

'Don't be afraid. That dog won't do a thing. It merely barks. Haven't you heard? Barking dogs seldom bite. I got it only to save myself from the nuisance of beggars. Its name is Appu. Who's this? Is he your son? In which class is he studying? What's his name?'

'Kaiser,' replied Ananthakrishnan. One more fistful of rice fell inside the bag. Reeking ration rice.

'Let's go home.'

Appukkuttan didn't quite recover from that shock. His face was pale as paper. He flinched from time to time. As they passed the gate, he tripped and fell.

'What's it, my dear?'

Appukkuttan was sobbing.

'Only eleven houses remain now. After that we can go home. If you can't walk, I'll carry you.'

Appukkuttan collapsed into his father's outstretched hands. His irises rolled upwards.

They couldn't complete the remaining eleven houses. Appukkuttan was down with a raging fever once again. Giving him medicine and pills, cooking rice gruel and feeding Appukkuttan, Ananthakrishnan was always by his side. He kept vigil during sweltering, windless nights, when not even a leaf stirred.

Nine

Kesavan too had had an experience similar to the one in which a dog had rushed in barking ferociously at Appukkuttan and his father as they entered the courtyard of the coir factory owner. A violent shock, first. Then, enervation....

But Kesavan welcomes such unexpected encounters. It's like the electric shock administered to the mentally ill. Although the shock startles and hurts you a bit, it also cures some minor ailments.

'You have lost a lot of weight, Kesavetta. Let's see a doctor.'

'You'll get such ideas when you sit idly.'

'It's not just a question of getting ideas. Look at yourself in the mirror, if you wish.'

When he went over and stood in front of the dressing mirror, he felt she had a point, after all. He is lean-built. Long hands. His index finger and middle finger are as long as pens. He says playfully that one day all his fingers will turn into pens.

Kesavan, who stood there after his bath, combing his hair, clad in a white mundu and ironed shirt, looked like the hero of one of those old black-and-white films directed by Sethumadhavan.

He was to change buses twice. And walk some distance after alighting from the bus. Sujatha didn't understand why he was going for Cheran's wedding, taking so much trouble. She tried to prevail upon him' saying that he mustn't go. Yet Kesavan was adamant and shrugged her off. Cheran is neither kith nor kin. Some acquaintance Kesavan once met somewhere and later on exchanged a couple of letters with. Cheran is a Dalit.

When the bus halted, there was the usual rush. Kesavan somehow got in through the door at the back and hung on. There wasn't space enough even for his feet to be planted on the floor. He was wonderstruck thinking how people like Moosath managed to travel in such buses. He was anxious about his dress, all white and ironed. He felt that it was better for the passengers if they too wore khaki uniforms like the bus conductors when travelling in buses. Khaki does not get easily soiled, even after being shoved and pushed around in a crowded bus.

The back of the bus stank of beedi-smoke and sweat. When the bus reached Attatheru, the stench of dry fish also would mingle with the odours of the laws. The winding, climbing Attatheru is a narrow street lined on both sides with dry fish shops. Disembowelled, salted sharks laid out to dry could also be seen here and there along the roadside. Moosath would never take that route. If at all he had to pass that way, he would cover his head and face with a towel.

As he bought the ticket and proceeded forward, jostling his way through the crowd, he extracted a faint fragrance from the air he inhaled. As he pressed ahead, the fragrance became denser. The dense scent of coconut oil on damp hair mingled with that of talcum powder. So the two ends of town-buses have two different worlds of smell. The back would always stink of beedi-smoke and dry fish. The front was filled with the fragrance of women's hair and cheeks.

Wherever he went, he would dilate his nostrils and catch scents. I must have been a dog in my previous birth, mused Kesavan. A police dog that had been scientifically trained to make out scents.

'Ayyo, saar…'

A woman who was sitting near where Kesavan was standing holding on to the bar in the ceiling of the bus, stood up. 'Please sit down, saar.'

She vacated her seat for him. It seemed that she had forgotten the fact that that seat was reserved for women. There was a sign of recognition, too, on her face. But he failed to recall who she was. Her dark face looked pale and tired. At the same time, her eyes retained some remnants of the sheen of youth.

'Sit down, saar,' she repeated.

'I am not a woman!'

Hearing that, someone nearby began to laugh. She felt embarrassed. Only then did she realise the confusion she had caused. It was a Muslim woman clad in a burqa who was sitting next to her. If Kesavan was to sit next to that woman…it could well have sparked off a communal riot.

The woman did not return to her seat. Instead, she stood next to him holding on to the bar above. Because of her short stature, it was difficult for her to stand like that.

'How did you recognise me?'

She merely smiled in reply. Now she was leaning dangerously close to him. Though he tried to move backward, he was unable to. He felt as if someone had put him in a cage. A cage made of human bodies, which was soft and cool.

'Where are you getting down, saar?'

'At the Old Bus Stand.'

'Oh, I too am getting down there.'

'Where is your house?'

'Beyond the rails. Six rupees by autorickshaw.'

'I have to catch another bus from the Old Bus Stand,' he informed her, even though she hadn't asked him. 'I am going to a wedding.'

He smiled without reason. The smile was rather incongruous with the white dress he was wearing. Kesavan would smile that kind of whitewash smile only very rarely.

How did she recognise me, he asked himself. Perhaps she was a devoted reader. She must have read all my novels and short-story collections. All of them carry my photograph on the back cover.

Whenever the bus braked or turned round a bend, he felt the softness of her body. Sometimes, he feared she was deliberately leaning towards him. Often, he shot furtive glances around to see whether anyone was watching them.

When the bus stopped in the Old Bus Stand, she too got down with him.

'Here's the bus to Balusseri. May I leave now?' He made to bid farewell and walk away. His white, ironed shirt was all crumpled. His neck and brow were covered with perspiration.

'Saar, it is one of my fondest wishes. Please grace my house with your presence, just once.'

The cleaner boy of the bus to Balusserri was hawking for passengers. If that bus left, he would have to wait a long time for another one.

'Some other time. I'll certainly come.'

'You'll never come. I know. You all are big people—,' she sounded offended.

Can I reach Cheran's house before the muhurtam, he wondered in anxiety. Two young men looked at him and whispered something as they crossed him. Walking a little distance, they turned around, looked at him and smiled disconcertingly. Everywhere readers recognise me nowadays, he thought. Like this woman recognised me in the bus. But the kind of awkwardness he detected in the eyes of the young men prompted him to surmise that they were not only readers but critics too.

She hailed an autorickshaw. When he sat in it, he felt a strange kind of security. He doesn't like to be a statue put up in a public place for everyone to look at. A little privacy, aloofness and an air of inscrutability...these are indispensable for a person like him. A writer should never be a direct kind of person. He should prowl around. He must play dark games. He must never stand in glaring light.

When the autorickshaw crossed over the railway track, the entire earth seemed to quake along with the vehicle. Beyond the rails, he saw a small reservoir from which water had dried up. There were green puddles of water here and there. Cows rested under a banyan tree on the banks of the reservoir.

'Don't compel me to drink tea and all that.... If you have any of my books, I'll autograph those. I have to reach Cheran's house before the muhurtam.'

She moved closer to him without uttering a word. She had been standing close to him in the bus. Perhaps female admirers behaved that way towards writers, he surmised.

The auto was now going along an empty road passing through stretches of uninhabited land. The driver shot forward without looking left or right. He had not asked where they were going. Perhaps the driver was her acquaintance, Kesavan thought.

The auto stopped in front of a small house that stood isolated in a vastly vacant area. The verandah had been enclosed by a wooden lattice screen. The house looked like a lion's cage.

'No one else is here?'

'Am I not enough?'

No light inside even during daytime. She switched on the light. A picture-calendar advertising a particular brand of brandy was hung on the wall. The picture of a girl standing all bare, white as lime. A chair, a small table with a sunmica top and a cot were there. She spread out the folded up mattress on the cot.

'Come, sit here.'

'Let me go now. If you want my autograph, bring me the book.'

'I don't have any book.'

'Take out a notebook, then. I'll sign on it.'

'I don't need your signature, saar. What's your name?'

Yanking out the hairpins that held her hair in a round bun, she undid her hair and let it fall freely over her shoulders.

'Don't be afraid. No one will come here. Just bolt that door, if you prefer it that way.'

'I'm off!'

He rushed towards the closed door. As he got out, sharp sunbeams pierced his eyes. She kept saying many things from behind him....

'How's Cheran's bride?' Sujatha asked Kesavan who had reached home earlier than expected.

'I didn't go for the wedding.'

Sujatha wasn't surprised. That was not the first time Kesavan returned home without reaching the destination. It was something peculiar about him.

Ten

'As a writer, you are such a hard-hearted man. Didn't that Thomaskunju fall at your feet begging you for a novel? Did you oblige him? Let it be. You didn't even try to mollify him with a word of comfort. Didn't you send him off like one of those beggars who come to you for alms on Saturdays? After all, isn't he the owner of a weekly with a print run of 50,000 copies?'

There was anger evident in Ravunni's tone. He continued, 'What is the difference between you and Thomaskunju? You make money by crafting words. He makes money by smearing ink on them. Tell me Kesavan, what is the difference between the two of you?'

'The difference is really between us and them,' Unni Kurup opined. 'We are the readers who buy words paying these people.'

Thomaskunju had come without prior notice. When he arrived, Kesavan was on his way to the latrine, carrying water in a plastic bucket.

'I am not in a hurry at all. Go, shit in peace and come back.'

Kesavan got into the latrine and closed the door keeping it ajar. The door didn't have a latch. The tiles above were cracked. Sujatha often reminds him to do up the latrine and to arrange for running water in it. But Kesavan doesn't like the idea of repairing anything. Let everything old remain the same way, Kesavan would say.

Thomaskunju sat on a chair in the verandah.

Sujatha appeared at the doorway and enquired after the well-being of Mariyamma Chedathi, Thomaskunju's wife, and the children. Then she went in to the kitchen to make tea.

Kesavan didn't emerge from the toilet even after twenty minutes.

'Kesava, I won't be fooled by your ruse. I know that you are avoiding me.' Thomaskunju said aloud standing in front of the latrine door. He had a booming voice. His baritone made it seem as though he was speaking out loud even when he spoke softly. What could it be like then if he actually spoke out loud?

'Save me, Kesavan. My weekly had touched the 100,000 mark. Now it is just half that number. If it goes on like this, I will have to go about with a beggar's bowl. My father was from Kottayam, the publisher's Mecca. So he died rich. It's our misfortune that Mariyamma and I migrated to this Kannur. With that, I lost the business instinct I inherited from my father. I have even forgotten the Kottayam variety of Malayalam! Look Kesavan, now I am speaking the lingo of you north Malabaris. Open the door and come out. You have shat enough. I have come with a deal. Don't you want to know what that is?'

There was not a stir from within the latrine. Not even a faint noise. Could there be a secret passage from that latrine, leading to some far-off place? Could Kesavan have escaped through it? Thomaskunju's suspicion turned to new directions. He wouldn't be surprised if Kesavan had actually escaped. Kesavan was an elusive, phantom-like writer.

'Kesavan, please give me that stuff you are writing about Eeyyemmess. If you do, my weekly and I will be saved. In return, I shall pull down the second storey of this ramshackle house and build a proper concrete floor. This is a deal struck never before between a writer and a publisher in this blessed land of ours.'

Kesavan opened the door and came out with the empty bucket, holding up the end of his mundu. His back was aching from having sat hunched over for a long time without moving.

'Are you happy with my deal, Kesavan?'

Thomaskunju looked at Kesavan up and down hopefully with his small, ferret-like eyes. His face bore the expression of an angler who had lowered his bait in river water.

Leaving the bucket by the well, Kesavan soaped and washed his hands, drew some water from the well and drank a couple of mouthfuls.

'Why don't you say something? Don't you feel even a bit of compassion towards this poor Thomaskunju?'

'I have nothing to say.'

'You don't have to say anything. Go, bring that novel and give it to me. I will put a concrete roof over your head before the monsoon.'

Kesavan had nothing to say.

Both sat in the verandah drinking the tea Sujatha had brought. Thomaskunju paraded many more temptations in front of Kesavan. That moment, he would have given whatever

Kesavan asked. If he had asked for the mythical parijata flower, Thomaskunju would have given him that as well. But not a single word escaped Kesavan's mouth. He sat there silently, as if he had swallowed his tongue. Finally, Thomaskunju bade adieu, cursing everyone including himself and rueing his fate.

'Kesavan, that publisher Thomaskunju is not a mere merchant. He is a lover of literature. That's why he sold off his father's 'Blade' company and started a weekly. You treated him heartlessly. You hid yourself like a thief in the latrine. I don't at all like this foul trick of yours.'

'I had already told him what I had to say.'

'Didn't you tell him that you had nothing to say?'

'Yes, that's what I had to say.'

'You will never mend your ways,' said Ravunni. Then, he called out in the direction of the kitchen: 'Sujatha, two cups of strong tea! For Unni and me.'

Ravunni and Unni Kurup had come there together.

There was no bag dangling from his shoulder. Neither a bottle of brandy, nor soda.

'After he stopped drinking, Ravunni Master has brightened up. Like a girl who has attained puberty,' commented Unni Kurup.

'Isn't the whole world changing? How then can drunkards not change? Some people don't like to change. You are one of them, Kesavan. The likes of you want to see me go about drunk, making a fool of myself. If it was not for this damned drinking, what heights I could have scaled! Wouldn't I have become the president of one of the Akademies, chairman of some government-owned corporations or at least a member of the Public Service

Commission? Aren't I qualified to become the Chairman of an organisation like the National Book Trust in Delhi? But I had never thought about my future, Kesavan. Like you, I too have a family. The eldest two of my children are girls of marriageable age. Shouldn't I think of them at least now? Thomaskunju's weekly has described me as the Gajakesari who succeeded Kesari. But I have never been able to offer even a little comfort to my poor wife. I, who came home every night stone-drunk after revelries, didn't even have the eye to see her body.'

'How else were four children born to you, then?'

'Didn't I say, Kesavan, you are heartless?!'

Unni Kurup, who was sitting as if in meditation, opened his eyes. While the others were talking, he was mentally in his classroom, lecturing. Years of teaching at the tutorial college have reduced him to this. Teaching his class mentally while walking or travelling in a bus is slowly becoming a habit with him.

'Ravunni Master has begun writing a smart article titled 'Existentialism in the Art of Colours'. It is a topic untouched by any Malayalam writer so far.'

'I am writing this article based on the works of Jonathan Lasker. If you have any material on Lasker's paintings, give them to me. I'll return them after my use.'

'Ayyo, I don't have anything with me.'

'Kesavan, you are slipping away like a catfish. Did you not write something about Lasker some eight years ago in a decrepit magazine run by some urchins from Palakkad?'

'I don't remember.'

'For you, even memory is a thing to be kept hidden. It is like black marketeers hoarding rice during a famine that you hide your memory and knowledge.'

'I have nothing with me. Even if it is there, it is impossible for me to look for it.'

'You don't do a thing. I'll take it upon myself to find out whatever you choose to hide.'

Ravunni walked to Kesavan's writing room to ransack his library. Kesavan was feeling out of depth, as though someone was trying to snatch away his toy. Ravunni continued rummaging in the library for quite some time and came back empty-handed. Ravunni had not known that hoarding knowledge was an art and that Kesavan had long since mastered that art.

'Why are you laughing, Kurup?'

'Nothing, Master.'

Kesavan tried to hoard knowledge; Ravunni was trying to loot it. Who is the criminal—the one who hoards or the one who loots? Unni Kurup asked himself.

'Dosa and tea are ready,' announced Sujatha.

Eleven

As Kesavan was sitting immersed in thought, his neighbour Aravindan came prowling in like a cat and stood beside him. Kesavan had been musing about Appukkuttan and Ananthakrishnan. A feeling that they were not merely characters but living persons was slowly taking root in him. Kesavan wouldn't be surprised if one day Ananthakrishnan came to his courtyard holding Appukkuttan's hand.

'Did you see this, Kesavetta?'

'I don't want to see anything.'

'This...'

'Didn't I say I didn't want to see anything? Nor do I want to see you. Be off!'

Aravindan continued to prowl around. He hasn't even bathed or brushed his teeth. He looked as if he had come straight from the mat he slept on. Aravindan's face bore a look as if he was carrying a cross unseen by others.

'I need only one minute. I will go. I won't disturb you, Kesavetta.' Aravindan looked at Kesavan miserably.

'Out with whatever damn thing you have to say.'

Aravindan spread the newspaper in his hand and showed it to Kesavan. It was that day's paper. Ravunni's photo was there right on the front page. Sharing the podium with the Chief Minister. The Chief Minister had an expression as if he had just drank some bitter concoction. But Ravunni was smiling, baring all his teeth. He was looking straight at the lens. People smile when they face the camera. And this smile of Ravunni was solely for the camera as well. The camera is the biggest buffoon the world has seen. It makes everyone laugh.

'Isn't he the one who comes to see you every so often?'

'Umm.'

'Ravunni Master?'

'Yes.'

'Tell Ravunni Master about me, please. He knows the Chief Minister. Some job for me...'

'There is also a mike before the Chief Minister. Is it enough if I recommend you to that mike?'

'Kesavetta...'

'The day hasn't dawned properly yet. And he has come with talk about his job. Hey, do you think that there's an employment exchange here?' Kesavan directed a look full of loathing at Aravindan. Aravindan stood there aghast' as if he had stepped on shit unawares.

'Go away from here. And never again set foot in this courtyard. Off with you!'

Aravindan folded up the paper, tucked it under his armpit and left. Kesavan was more incensed at his cadaverous facial expression. Why can't he laugh at least sometimes? Why can't he walk briskly swinging his hands?

'Hey, stop.'

Kesavan went in, took out some money from his shirt pocket and came back.

'Go for a movie in town. There is a blockbuster action film of Amitabh Bachchan playing in Chitravani. Watch that one.'

He thrust the money in the palm of the hesitant Aravindan. He stood around for some more time, not knowing what to do.

'What else do you want now? Didn't you get the money? Can't you go now?'

Later, Kesavan watched Aravindan slinking away along the path in a pair of trousers.

'You never take me to a movie,' Sujatha said dourly.

'Who said he is going for a movie? He will get into one of those bars and come back drunk. Just you watch. I am unable to find jobs for the likes of him. Give them some money for a couple of drinks and help them forget the rigours of unemployment. That's all I can do.'

He unfolded the day's newspaper that was lying on the pyol. Kesavan had not seen it yet. I was not the same one that Aravindan had spread before him, but it also carried Ravunni's photo. A colour photo of him with the Chief Minister.

Kesavan already knew that Ravunni, who was a member of the Executive Committee of the Academy of Letters, had gone to Delhi by the morning flight from Kozhikode. His intention was not only to participate in the Executive Committee meeting but also to examine two Jonathan Lasker originals in the possession of an American diplomat. He was bent on seeing some Lasker paintings in order to give a modernist character to his essay 'Existentialism and the Art of Colours'.

'For whom are you writing this essay?'

'For Thomaskunju. He insists on people like me to write for him to help change the 'pulp' character of his weekly.'

Kesavan doesn't write anything nowadays. He is trying to forget EMS and Appukkuttan. He hates the characters of his novel—Appukkuttan, Ananthakrishnan and the rest. He can remember them only with loathing. His own characters are becoming a burden. Zooming in, buzzing and biting like mosquitoes, they wreck his sleep. He realises with a start that none of his characters has ever given him any happiness. What is the use of these vermin-like characters he gave shape to, forgoing food and sleep? Who has any use for them? Are they at least worth the cost of paper and ink that go into launching them into the world?

Thinking along these lines, Kesavan sat on the verandah, his legs outstretched. In between his toes, there were marks left by ringworm. Raising his mundu above his knees, he looked at his legs, as if he was seeing them for the first time.

An open grey umbrella passed along the lane.

'What's it, Kesavan?'

'Nothing.'

'Are you on leave today too?'

'Took a day more.'

'What's special?'

'Is anything 'special' necessary, to avail leave?'

'Ayyo, I didn't mean it that way....'

Moosath hurried along with his umbrella and bag.

Kesavan had availed of leave today to mull over a few things.

How was Kesavan to address Appukkuttan? Father called him 'Appu'. Mother called him 'Kuttan.' And the people,

'Appukkuttan.' Wouldn't he be taking the side of the people if he called him 'Appukkuttan?' Kesavan doesn't like to take anyone's side. Maybe he could call him 'Kuttappan.' In it are his father's 'Appu', mother's 'Kuttan' and the people's 'Appukkuttan.'

Kuttappan.

Kesavan chuckled to himself at the erotic innuendo in the name.

Kesavan considers naming characters a very difficult business. It was after long and sustained deliberation that he had decided to christen the hero of his new novel 'Appukkuttan'. The story was set in a village in north Malabar. The name 'Appukkuttan' was not a familiar one in that area at all. Kesavan had walked the length and breadth of that village, like a census official, enquiring whether there was anyone named 'Appukkuttan', especially a child. Most of the names ended with 'esh': Jithesh, Jitheesh, Deepesh, Prabhesh, Sudheesh, Sumesh, Sukesh, Dhanesh...and so on.

Kesavan chose the name 'Appukkuttan' not because he was particularly fond of it. He could not find another name that the father and the mother called differently and the people completed. He had carried the name 'Balakrishnan' in his mind for some time.

Mother called him 'Balan'. Father called him 'Krishnan.' And the people, 'Balakrishnan.'

Thus it was the people who made him complete....

Kesavan once tried writing it thus. And immediately he discarded the name. Because the distance between 'Balan' and 'Krishnan' was evident. There is no such distance between 'Appu' and 'Kuttan' in 'Appukkuttan.'

It was not only during the writing of the new novel that the exercise of naming his characters had troubled Kesavan. Sometimes it had brought about grave dangers too. When his novel *The Gaze of a Frog* was being serialised in Thomaskunju's weekly, he had reached the very brink of one such disaster.

In that novel, there had been an old man called Kunhambu, who pulled the eight-year-old girl of his neighbours onto his lap whenever he got a chance. It was when the first chapter was already in press that Kesavan remembered that his grandfather's name was Kunhambu. His mother had told him how he would sit on the shoulder of grandpa Kunhambu and playfully pull his gold ear-studs. She also told him that grandpa had been very fond of him and that he would regularly buy toys and sweets for Kesavan. But Kesavan could not even remember the face of his grandfather, who had died when he was very young.

If the novel were published with his grandpa's name for that character, the curse and wrath of all the feminists in the country would fall on Kunhambu. The very name Kunhambu would become the symbol of child abuse.

Would poor grandpa Kunhambu's soul rest in peace in such an eventuality?

Without even waiting to change his shirt and mundu, Kesavan caught the first bus to Thomaskunju's office.

'What is it Kesavan, have you come for getting some advance payment? Should you have come all the way to this place in this scorching sun, in a jampacked bus? You could have just telephoned. O, you don't have a phone at home. We can arrange a connection for you. If there is no phone in the house of a writer like you, it is the telephone department that stands to lose in prestige. All right. What do you want, cheque or cash? I hear that you are a gentleman who doesn't evade tax. Still, I can arrange cash...'

'It is not for money that I came. I have inadvertently depicted my grandfather as a child molester. I have to make a correction.'

'Do you think your dead grandfather would ever read this nondescript weekly of mine?'

'I haven't come here to argue with you. I want to change my grandpa's name.'

Sitting in the weekly's office, Kesavan changed the name 'Kunhambu' to 'Achuthan' throughout the manuscript, over two cups of tea.

After another cup of tea, he caught the Payyannur Fast Passenger bus back home. What he did not remember when he sat dozing off in the bus was that Sujatha's granduncle's name was Achuthan. Achuthammavan, Uncle Achuthan.

Twelve

'Where does rain come from?'

'From the clouds.'

'How are clouds formed?'

'By water turning into vapour.'

'How does water turn into vapour?'

'By the sun's heat.'

'Will we too turn into vapour if we get the sun's heat?'

'No.'

'Why is that?'

'Only water turns into vapour.'

'Why is that?'

There is no beginning or end to the queries of Appukkuttan, who wants to know everything. Running within the circles of questions, Ananthakrishnan soon grew exhausted.

Ananthakrishnan cannot understand why Appukkuttan is so curious to learn everything. He hasn't noticed any other children asking such questions of their parents, perplexing them. If Sreedevi was alive, he could have escaped the load of half the questions, handling them over to her.

What does Appukkuttan gain by asking questions this way? Hey Appootta, have you set out to write an encyclopaedia at this tender age? If so, forget it. I will educate you only upto BA. You must not study beyond that. After your graduation, I'll get you the job of a clerk, begging or bribing someone, if need be. In a government office. So, you must go to the office every day, wearing trousers, a pair of hawai chapals on your feet and a ballpoint pen in your pocket. You need to have only a small-time life like that. If you are going to trouble me with big ambitions, I'll send you to your mother's side. That's the place fit for those who have a lot of dreams and ambitions. I live on like this here because I don't have any of those anymore.

Appukkuttan must be told a story if he is to go to sleep; that is the norm. Ananthakrishnan knows that it is just a ruse and that Appukkuttan can very well go to sleep without listening to a story. Still he will say,

'Father. Tell me a story. Sleep is not coming near me.'

When he says this, his eyes are almost shut with sleep. The crook!

Are stories meant to be sleep-inducing? Are stories sleeping pills? Stories are meant to awaken the mind. It is from the stories we listen to in our parents' lap or lying in bed that a sense of ethics and morality and justice develops in us.

But Ananthakrishnan's problem was none of that.

'Let Appu decide for himself whether he should lead a life of morals or develop a sense of justice, when he grows up. I am not going to advise him on any of that. I have put him in school not to give him knowledge or education, d'you hear? It is just to get a degree when he grows up. Just for that piece of paper. What job will you get without that piece of paper? How'll Appu live? D'you understand what I say?'

The Two Drunks nodded.

This is Ananthakrishnan's problem:

How to tell Appukkuttan new stories everyday? Long ago, Ananthakrishnan's mind was full of stories and knowledge. There was an undrying udder of stories within him. But he has forgotten everything. Like wiping out the words written on a slate using the sap of a succulent stem, he wiped out his past.

'All my ambitions and dreams are gone. Knowledge and story vanished together with that. Now nothing is left. Except this body...'

'Alas!' said the Two Drunks.

Fathers build the future of their children with their own past. On what foundation will Ananthakrishnan build the future of Appukkuttan, with his non-existent past?

Therefore, he would tell his son:

'Hey Appu. We don't need a great future. A small education. A small job. A small house... We need only these.'

As Ananthakrishnan sat troubled, all his old stories running out of stock, Vettom Mani (the editor and compiler of Puranik Encyclopaedia) appeared in a vision. He said, with deep compassion,

'Ananthakrishnan, do not be troubled. It is for the likes of you that I wrote Puranik Encyclopaedia. Buy one copy. You'll get it at an economy price in the pre-publication scheme.'

It was years since Ananthakrishnan had bought a book. Not only books; he didn't even buy or read weeklies or newspapers for that matter.

He bought a copy of Puranic Encyclopaedia for Appukkuttan. He got the Rs 250/- book at forty percent discount. The smell of the book aroused in him some forgotten memories. His school and college days. Those days when he sat nights on end reading the books he borrowed from the library....

'What book is this, Father?'

'Stories.'

'What stories?'

'All sorts of stories.'

'Even Eeyyemmess's story?'

Appukkuttan's face brightened.

Ananthakrishnan mused: It's not my brother Ramkakrishan, it's I who am responsible for this obsession of Appu with Eeyyemmess. As soon as Appu was born, that blood-hued picture of Eeyyemmes should have been removed and replaced with one of Bhagavan Sree Krishna, Sathya Sai Baba, or some film star. There was no dearth of pictures, printed and supplied from Sivakasi. He remembered the pictures of Siva and Parvathy, Subramanya Swamy and Muttappan on sale on the stalls during the festival of Muttappan at Parassinikkadavu Mathappura. Those pictures were available at a reduction price on wholesale or retail.

Or, shouldn't it have been enough if I had moved the cradle away from EMS's picture?

At that time, no such idea had entered Ananthakrishnan's head. He had not known that EMS would ooze down into Appukkuttan as he lay playing, moving his limbs in the cradle, or with the feeding bottle on his lips or snoozing with the froth of milk in the corners of his mouth.

Ananthakrishnan was confused as to whether it was the Communist Party Office or Sree Muttappan's temple, at Parassinikkadavu, when he went to see the Vellattu. Because red flags were fluttering wherever his eyes took him.

'Why is it Father, that there are so many dogs here?

'Because the dog is Muttappan's vehicle.'

'What's a vehicle?'

'A vehicle is…'

'A bus is called a vehicle. So dogs are Muttappan's buses?'

Ananthakrishnan didn't have an answer.

Dogs were seen jostling their way through the crowds. In vacant corners they had curled up, dozing off.

Eating boiled gram and coconut slivers and drinking hot tea to accompany that, father and son watched the Vellattu.

Appukkuttan's choroonu was conducted at Mathappura. Every year after that, Ananthakrishnan would go there regularly, along with Appukkuttan. And offer Payankutty a ritual offering of arrack, dried fish, boiled gram and coconut slivers in a coconut shell made to Parassinikkadavu Muthappen. And eat hot rice with dried fish curry sitting in the temple yard along with other devotees. Buying a toy for Appukkuttan, he would climb down the hill that reeked of over-ripe cashew apple scent, and catch the bus to Kannur.

'Hey Appu, don't you want a toy now?' asked Ananthakrishnan as they returned after offering worship.

All along the way were hawkers selling all kinds of toys and playthings. Painted clay parrots, rubber balls, toy-bugles and balloons…

Even during Ananthakrishnan's childhood, the same toys were sold there. The hawkers change; toys are the same.

'Hey Appu, shall we buy a pair of parrots? Look, how pretty they are! We shall put them on either side of the time-piece on the wall, shall we?

Appukkuttan didn't say a thing.

He walked along holding tight his father's hand so that he wouldn't get lost in the crowd. The biggest rush was in front of shops where mirrors, combs, bangles, collyrium etc were sold. The women who thronged there smelt of sweat and powder.

'We'll buy a ball then; we can play with it in the evenings in the courtyard.'

'I don't want a ball.'

'What do you want, then?'

'The photo of Eeyyemmess.'

'Hey, this is Muttappan's temple. You won't get Eeyyemmess's photo here.'

Would I buy it for you, even if it was available here? One picture has brought about so much of trouble. If yet another picture is hung in the house...

'Walk now. We don't want either Eeyyemmes...or his photo. And you won't get the photo here either.'

'The photo is just there.'

Appukkuttan took his father's hand and led him forward through the crowds. Knocking and pushing, shooing and jostling, he took his father forward. On both sides of the path were stalls. Stalls where baskets, murams, mat, etc were sold. Stalls where plastic buckets and basins were sold. Stalls where china bowls, plates and glasses were sold. Everywhere, people were crowding in front of the stalls.

'Appu, where are you dragging me to?'

'Here, look! Eeyyemmess's photo,' he pointed.

It was a stall that exhibited rows upon rows of pictures of Muttappan, Sree Narayana Guru, Sai Baba and MGR. Among the pictures of gods and filmstars, a picture of EMS was also there. EMS who smiles innocently like a child, wearing thick glasses. Though his head is full of deep and grave thoughts, EMS's smile is like a child's. Not even Appukkuttan, who is a child, can smile so guilelessly.

Women who had come from Coorg bought Muttappan's pictures in bulk. Those pictures would from now on adorn their homes and the buses and lorries their husbands drove.

'Appu, we won't buy that. Haven't we got a photo of Eeyyemmess at home? That's enough.'

'I want this too.'

'That's not for sale. It's hung there, like we have in our house. Come, I'll buy a pair of clay parrots for you. They'll look nice on either side of the timepiece on the wall. Come...'

Appukkuttan stood there immobile, as if he had dropped anchor.

'Won't you come away?'

'No.'

'Don't come, then. I am going. Are you trying to turn my house into a Party Office? Don't try that one on me.'

He walked forward through the crowds. After moving a little away when he looked back, Appukkuttan was coming after him, sulking.

'Appukkuttan will buy Eeyyemmess's photo, after growing up and getting a job. A hundred photos,' Appukkuttan said, sitting in the bus.

'My prayer is that my eyes should close forever, before that happens.'

Ananthakrishnan sat looking outside. Buses that rush back and forth are filled with Muttappan's devotees. There were women, old men and children. In the hands of almost all there were packets, big or small. Those who go to worship Muttappan don't return empty-handed. They would at least buy pots or pans. It's only Ananthakrishnan and Appukkuttan who return empty-handed.

'Appu.'

'Don't talk to me.'

The still-sulking Appukkuttan turned his face away.

Thirteen

From Appukkuttan's house, it is not even a mile to his school. Everyday he went to school walking. Once The Two Drunks asked why Ananthakrishnan was not sending Appukkuttan to school in an autorickshaw. Let his legs get tough from walking, was Ananthakrishnan's reply.

The Two Drunks were very exhausted. The previous night a battle had raged between Saravanan and the two of them, under the culvert. The battle was for the right to sit on the parapet wall of that culvert. Though The Two Drunks were healthier than Saravanan, they lost the battle. It was with his tongue that Saravanan defeated them. Thus Saravanan firmed up his right to sit on the parapet wall of that culvert. And the fame of Saravanan's tongue spread far and wide.

Appukkuttan would walk alone till the Taluk Office. He had to go past the culvert. At the spot where The Two Drunks sat, Saravanan was sitting now. The shade of the kanjiram tree was spread all around. On the wall at one side of the culvert, film posters were displayed.

Near the Taluk Office, Vasudevan, Appukkuttan's classmate, and his younger sister Padmavathy, would join him. Padmavathy was in class one.

'Appukkuttan, you are so brave,' Padmavathy would say as she walked alongside him. 'How do you manage to walk all alone along the alleyway? What would you do if a cow appeared?'

What would he do if a cow appeared from the opposite side as he was walking along the alley? Thinking about that, Padmavathy started. There wouldn't be enough space for the cow to pass. One would have to press close to the mud wall and make place for the cow. If the cow so much as shook its head as it passed, wouldn't its horn gore one's stomach?

'I am not afraid of cows.'

'Appukkuttan, aren't you afraid of anything in the world?'

'No.'

'I am afraid of everything; of the cow too.'

'Aren't you a girl? That's why.'

She is afraid of cows, lightning, rain, Saravanan and the one-legged Pokker.

Pokker, who arrives regularly for alms on Saturdays, is not to be seen nowadays. But Saravanan is found at the bus stop in the junction, in front of the Post Office, and, sometimes, in the precincts of the school. After defeating The Two Drunks in battle, he is now seen sitting on the culvert everyday.

'He's a bad one,' said Padmavathy. 'Always pees on the road. He thinks that he's still a child.'

When he was walking to school alone on Thursday, he saw Saravanan. He was sitting on the culvert smoking a bidi. It would be more accurate to say that Saravanan saw Appukkuttan. He was so thin that it seemed he would fly away, if one blew hard. Appukkuttan could never understand why Padmavathy was fearing such a person.

'Hey kid! Who are you?'

Appukkuttan didn't at all like that 'kidding.' He walked straight ahead pretending not to notice him.

'What's your name?'

Appukkuttan didn't even acknowledge that he had heard the question.

'Aren't you that Ananthakrishnan's son?'

'Umm.'

'Your father is a cheat.'

Appukkuttan bent down, picked up a stone and threw it at Saravanan. The stone flew past Saravanan's nose. Though he threw the stone from such close quarters, the stone didn't hit the target. Appukkuttan is a bad thrower.

Vasudevan is an expert at throwing. Standing at the school gate, he can hit the lamp-post at the opposite side of the road. When he once hit the post thus, the bulb dropped from the lamp and burst on the ground.

'Scram.'

Vasudevan ran. Appukkuttan and Padmavathy too ran. Padmavathy asked as she ran, 'Will the police catch us?'

She was weeping.

For two full days she cowered in dread of the police. She started awake dreaming about policemen. Earlier she would start awake dreaming about cows.

'Father, are you a cheat?'

'What's it, Appu? Are you drunk?'

Suddenly Appukkuttan saw light. Everyone who was a drunkard would feel that his father was a cheat. Isn't it because he is a drunkard that Saravanan said so? No one who was not a drunk had so far told Appukkuttan that his father was a cheat.

'Who told you that?'

'Saravanan, the drunkard.'

'Why did you stop to talk to him? Do you stop on the road and talk to all and sundry when you go to school?' Ananthakrishnan was incensed.

It was during the walk from home to school and back that Appukkuttan learned everything. That walk, which was less than a mile, would be more useful than a long journey. The path between the house and the school was his main blood vessel. It was on that path that he met Saravanan for the first time. At one side of the alley, the mud wall had caved in. He could reach Chathu Maestry's house easily, if he took the shortcut through the breach in the wall. Once, he chanced upon Maistry's daughter Kamala and the tailor Ramanan standing behind the broken wall, holding hands. It was Padmavathy, a couple of years younger than him, who told him that it was 'love' between Ramanan and Kamala. Another time when he was returning from school he found a faded wallet lying on the road at the bend near the Taluk Office. In that purse reeking of tobacco, so many things were stuffed. It contained twelve rupees and some change, besides.

'Let's buy ellunda with it,' Vasudevan said, 'And drink soda too.'

'No. Let's go for a movie,' said Padmavathy. A newly released film featuring Jayan and Ranichandra was on her mind.

'Ayyo, no!' Appukkuttan said. 'This is not our money.'

Appukkuttan ran home with the money. He handed over the purse to his father.

'Did you take some money from this?'

'No.'

'Swear.'

'I haven't taken any money from it. I swear upon Eeyyemmess.' Appukkuttan swore.

Ananthakrishan felt very happy. At the same time, he also felt some anxiety. If it was any other child, he would either have bought some eatable with the money, or hidden it away. Will Appukkuttan be able to live on in a world full of deception and falsehood, if he were so straight and honest? Shouldn't he have a bit more of practical sense?

That was Moosath's purse. Ananthakrishnan immediately went over to Moosath's Matham and handed it over to him.

'Ananthakrishnan, may your son be blessed,' Moosath showered his benediction on Appukkuttan.

But the next day Vasudevan quarrelled with Appukkuttan.

'You are a buffalo,' said Vasudevan. Who would return money that was lost-and-found?

For two days Appukkuttan and Vasudevan did not speak to each other. Padmavathy didn't take anyone's side. Her conscience told her that what Appukkuttan had done was right. She also felt that Vasudevan shouldn't have called Appukkuttan, a 'buffalo'. But, when all was said and done, Vasudevan was her elder brother. So she didn't speak out in support Appukkuttan. She walked along with them, without saying anything.

There were four shops after the Taluk Office. Ramanan's tailoring shop was one. Kamala's brother Rajan was standing there, talking with Ramanan. Rajan cadged a beedi from Ramanan, lit it and blew out the smoke. In one hand Rajan held a rolled up poster and in the other, a tin can full of gum.

'Is it a film poster?' Padmavathy asked eagerly. 'Could you give me one?'

'Isn't your father a Congressman? Go away.'

Padmavathy was suddenly sad. And angry.

'The cow will tear you apart you. Just you watch.' Padmavathy cursed Rajan vehemently.

Appukkuttan had the suspicion earlier on that Padmavathy's father was a Congressman, because he went about wearing khadi. But subsequently he learned that he was not a member of the Congress Party always. Because Appukkuttan had seen him going about wearing something other than khadi many a time.

Without taking the smoking beedi off his lips, Rajan hitched up his lungi above his thigh, tucked it at the waist, and began to apply gum on the back of the poster. Vasudevan, Padamavathy and Appukkuttan stood looking at the poster lying face down. Padmavathy was sure that it would be Jayan and Rani Chandra on the poste. Turning the poster around, Rajan stuck it on the outer wall of Ramanan's shop. It was the picture of an old man wearing thick glasses. There was the hammer and sickle on one top corner of the poster. Seeing this, Padmavathy was very much put down. But, Appukkuttan's happiness knew no bounds.

Looking at the poster, the gum still wet, Appukkuttan read out: EMS speaks at the Fort Maidan.

'Where is the Fort Maidan?'

Rajan, who was wiping away the gum from his fingers, turned and looked at him.

'At Kannur.'

'Where is Kannur?'

'Some distance away. You can go there by bus. And by train, too. The jail which houses thieves and murderers is in Kannur.'

'Will they put Eeyyemmess also in the jail?'

'Which police has the guts to do that? If anyone touches a single hair of Eeyyemmess, this land will go up in flames.'

Rajan walked over to the other shop with rolled up posters and gum.

'Appootta, are you coming along? The bell will go now. O! My God!'

Padmavathy shouted. Vasudevan had already left. She was afraid to go alone. There was a butting cow in Kunhiraman Master's house. She had to pass that house.

When Appukkuttan walked up, she moved alongside him.

As they neared Kunhiraman Master's house, she slowed down and Appukkuttan went ahead. She could see the cow standing in the shed, from a long way off. Suddenly she darted away like an arrow leaving the bow. She stopped running only after passing five houses, including the one next to Kunhiraman Master's. Appukkuttan was far behind.

Fourteen

One day, an elderly woman approached the compound, entered through the gate and walked upto Kesavan's house. It was Lakshmi Teacher. She held her umbrella open to escape the sun. She was not like Visalakshmi Ezhuthamma, who was also a teacher. She was tall and had a beautiful physique. Since Lakshmi Teacher was from another region, Moosath could not steal her height. In her locality, there are no lurking Moosaths who steal the heights of lady teachers.

'Is no one here?'

Lakshmi Teacher said aloud, without folding the umbrella. Shaking away the gravel that was caught between the soles of her feet and the chappal, she waited for someone to open the door.

Sujatha was straining the cooked rice. Wiping the sweat off her brow with the hem of her sari, she peeped into the courtyard. It was the fourth visitor for Kesavan, after daybreak. It was not yet noon. How many more were to come, she wondered. She had planned to take a bath, after setting the pot of rice to strain. Her body was covered with perspiration, as if the sun was shining inside the house as well. Her plan to have a bath was wrecked. Because of her husband's literary activities, she was not even able to take a bath! By the time she got into the bathroom and bolted the door, someone would call out from the courtyard. So many times she had come running, wrapping her sari around her body, wiped dry before the soap's lather was properly washed away.

'Don't let anyone into the house. Don't open the door, whoever comes. I will keep a dog that bites, if it comes to that,' Kesavan often says.

'Ayyo! Aren't they your readers? They come to you out of their admiration for you, don't they?'

'No one need admire me. Let the readers sit quietly at home and read. There is no need for them to disturb me, coming here all the way in a bus or auto.'

Kesavan is one who doesn't hesitate to do what he says. He may tether not merely a biting dog, but even a lion in the courtyard.

On the other hand, she can never act as she feels in her mind. She is very brave inside. And very timid outside.

'Isn't this Kesavan's house?'

'Yes.'

'Is Kesavan in?'

'He has gone to cut his hair.'

'Will he come back soon?'

'Yes. Please come in and sit down.'

Shutting the umbrella, Lakshmi Teacher entered the verandah. There were beads of perspiration on her brow and neck.

Though her hair was all-white, youthfulness had not entirely drained away from her visage. Her laughter and voice were like that of a young woman.

'Do you know me, Sujatha?'

'No.'

'I am Lakshmi Teacher. Retired last month as Principal of Sree Narayana College.'

'Please sit down, Teacher.'

Keeping the chappals in the outer verandah, she took her seat in the chair.

'As I have retired, now I have a lot of free time to meet my favourite writers and talk to them. It has been my long-cherished desire to meet Kesavan. That is to be fulfilled today!'

Sujatha prayed inwardly that Kesavan, who had gone for a haircut, should soon come back.

Standing at the door, she looked at her wet hands and soiled sari. The inner skirt with a torn hem could be seen beneath the sari. What will Teacher think? Are they the kind of clothes to wear, in front of visitors?

Even God can't say when Kesavan will return, once he goes out. On one occasion, he went out in the morning to post a letter, and he came back only in the afternoon.

'You may be busy in the kitchen, Sujatha. Go on, I'll wait here till Kesavan returns.'

'What would you like to drink...?'

'A glass of kanjivellam. With a little salt. Not too much of it. I have high blood pressure.'

Lakshmi Teacher smiled. Seeing that smile, Sujatha felt that she must have been a great beauty in her youth. There was a clear incongruity between Teacher's white hair and her sexy smile. She asked herself why Teacher did not dye her hair. She would look, maybe, thirty if she dyed her hair. Thirty-five at the most.

She drank the kanjivellam Sujatha brought, blowing into it to cool it down. As she drank half a glass, sweat began to flow down in rivulets from her throat.

'You have only one son, yes?'

'Umm.'

'Isn't his name Satheesan?'

'You know everything, Teacher.'

'He maybe as intelligent as his father. And brilliant in studies.'

'Of course, he has his father's intelligence. That's why he failed last year.'

'Many like me must be coming here, no? You may not have any peace and quiet. That's how it is when you are the wife of a celebrity. Yet you are so fortunate, Sujatha. When I went to my son's bedroom at daybreak once to cover him properly, I found a book on his chest. He had fallen asleep reading it. It was one of Kesavan's books. How many more would be sleeping thus, with your husband's book on their chests... I feel envious of you.'

'Do you too sleep like that, Teacher? With Kesavettan's book on your chest?'

Teacher was embarrassed at that question. Suddenly tossing a pretty smile, Teacher continued:

'I only said you are fortunate, Sujatha.'

'You see only the good points. There are things none of you get to see. There are people who spit on Kesavettan's books. Sometime ago, an aged man came upto this courtyard, and spat out. And cursed, 'Kesavan, may your life go to the dogs.' You don't know about any of that, Teacher.'

'Oh my Sujatha, there are also things you don't know, but I know.'

'What do you know? Tell me, whatever it is.'

Sujatha who was standing at the door so far, moved closer to where Teacher was, and sat down. What does she have to say? Is it the story of some college girl who has a crush on Kesavan? Or a story of this crush developing into infatuation? What's new about that...she has already heard so many such stories...

'For quite some time, some of Kesavan's books were on our syllabus. It was I who taught them all. Once reading Kesavan's book, a girl...'

'Enough Teacher. Say no more. The rest I can imagine.'

'Please listen to the rest of it, Sujatha. One day, on Kesavan's photo on the back cover, there was a red dot. With blood... That wasn't ordinary blood. I heard of it from the other girls.'

'Did you let her off, then, Teacher?'

'What could I say? How can I offer advice to a girl studying in the MA class?'

Drinking up the remaining kanjivellam, Teacher took out a kerchief from the folds of her sari at the waist and wiped her face, neck and hands. Sujatha noticed that Teacher's stomach had not lost its sheen or colour, despite her age.

Teacher continued:

'It's not for telling you all this that I came here, Sujatha. I had intended to meet Kesavan just once and then go away. But I don't know why all this tumbled out of me. I'll go now. You may have a lot of work in the kitchen. I can come back any time now. Aren't I the retired Principal? With a lot of free time.'

As Teacher made to get up, Sujatha made her sit down again.

'Don't go. Kesavattan will come back just now.'

Teacher sat down again. The salted kanjivellam had slaked her thirst. Though the sun was sweltering outside, an occasional cool breeze came into the verandah. Teacher's sweat dried up.

Sujatha somehow felt a liking towards Lakshmi Teacher. She forgot about the work in the kitchen and her bath.

They continued their conversation, sitting in the midday breeze. Teacher was talking without any order or structure. She began talking about the migration of Christians into Wynad, and then began talking about Kunchan Nambiar's sex life. Like the pieces on a chessboard, the topics of conversation kept racing here and there. Like the chess pieces moved to a strict code of rules, Teacher's topics also seemed to be following some unseen rules. Migration and Kunchan Nambiar may share an invisible bond. Like, both words kudiyettam (migration) and Kunchan Nambiar began with 'Ku.'

'There is a good film playing at Chitravani. Doesn't Kesavan take you for movies?

'Yes. He took us for a movie three months ago. Do you want to listen to that story?'

Sujatha described that incident to Lakshmi Teacher.

That day Kesavan reached home early, in an autorickshaw. As he was stepping on to the verandah, he said:

'I know that I am not fulfilling my responsibilities towards you as a husband, Sujatha. I am not at all paying attention to any of your concerns. You have a lot of work to do in the kitchen. Help Satheesan with his homework. Make tea for the zany who come to see me. And even make rice and curry sometimes, for some. Would that Ravunni, Pavithran and Unni Kurup go away without eating a meal of rice and curry whenever they come here? I don't even inquire whether the money I give you is enough for subsistence, at the least. I fail to see your difficulties, amidst my troubles. But none of this is intentional. You, who have lived with me for so long, surely know that. Anyway, I am going to take you for a movie today. That's why I have returned early from office. Wear that almost-black sari and put a black dot on your brow. We won't get tickets for the matinee show if we don't leave early.'

'Enough,' said Sujatha to him. 'Say the rest after getting inside the house.'

He got inside the house.

'Do you know, Teacher. I didn't have an almost-black sari. Never had even a black sari.'

Sujatha got ready. Satheesan too was readied. The auto-rickshaw was waiting in the lane.

Thus, Kesavan and family went for a movie together after a very long time. Sujatha was very, very happy.

'But Teacher, as we reached the town, Kesavettan's mind changed.'

'Don't get me wrong, Sujatha.' Kesavan said, in a low voice, sitting in the auto. 'We can go for a film some other time. Now let's go to the Coffee House, have a coffee and ghee-roasted dosa each and catch the breeze at the beach.'

'At this high noon?'

'I don't want coffee,' Satheesan said. 'I want Faluda. And I want to see the film as well.'

'My son was very insistent, Teacher. Yet, Kesevettan's mind didn't change. Finally nothing happened, Teacher. No film. No ghee-roasted dosas. No breeze at the beach. We returned home in the same auto.'

Teacher laughed: 'Writers are strange characters, Sujatha. They don't think or act like we do. Isn't that why they become writers?'

'All that is a lot of pretence, Teacher. Aren't writers human beings? Can't they behave like others? It's all play-acting... That day I felt like killing Kesavettan...'

Sujatha went on:

'Kesevettan is always like that. He never finishes what he begins. Doesn't reach where he is supposed to. That is his habit. You can see that for yourself right now, Teacher. Hasn't he gone to crop his hair? Just watch. He will come back without getting his haircut.'

She was so sure of that. Kesavan wouldn't have reached anywhere near the hair-cutting saloon. He would be drinking tea in Kannan's tea shop at the junction. Or, he may be standing at the bus stop looking at passers-by, exchanging pleasantries with them.

'He has developed a new habit over the past few days. He won't drink the tea I make. For that he has to go to Kannan's tea shop at the junction.'

Hearing a rustling sound outside the gate, Sujatha looked in that direction hurriedly, thinking that it might be Kesavan. It was some passer-by. All passers-by would look towards the house. She had been prevailing upon Kesavan for a long time to take down the fence and build a high wall in its place...

Sujatha continued:

'There are many more stories like the movie incident, Teacher. There will be no end to it. Be that as it may. You haven't said anything about your husband. What's he doing?'

'After retirement, he is going about with social reformation activities of the Sree Narayana Dharma Paripalana Sangam and all that. He is fifteen years older than I am. I am not yet through with enjoying life. And he has become so senile. Oh my God! What am I blurting out! Sujatha! Please do not take me wrong…'

It was after retirement that Lakshmi Teacher began talking like this. When she was still teaching, she was very circumspect about her speech. Would keep a dignified air about her talk, conduct and movements. But as soon as she retired, she declared independence. It was her tongue that declared independence first.

'He has only the SNDP to talk about, always. He has dedicated himself to its work for the last fifteen years or so.' Teacher continued, 'Have you seen Narayana Guru's photograph as a young man? Any woman would readily fall in love with the Guru.'

'No one will ever get the life one dreams about.'

Sujatha looked out. Only after Kesavan returned would she take a bath and change her sari.

'I know that you have a lot of work, Sujatha. Go on to the kitchen and carry on with your work. I'll sit here.' Teacher said. 'I'll just have a glimpse of Kesavan, touch the hand that holds the pen and then go away.'

It was then that a shadow moved beyond the fence. Kesavan walked in, hurriedly. He had had a haircut. And a shave.

Fifteen

Kesavan finalised a title for his new novel after turning it over and over in his mind for a long time—*Appukkuttan's Lamentations.*

Kesavan was not fully satisfied with the title. Yet, he decided that he would not change it.

Before he began writing the novel, he had had a title in mind. He had changed it even before the first chapter was completed. When he reached Chapter Four, that title gave way to yet another. He had given seven such titles to his novel so far. But *Appukkuttan's Lamentations* will not change, he has resolved.

On the first page of the manuscript, right on top, in the empty space, he wrote in large letters, 'Appukkuttan's Lamentations'. In order to avoid another title-change, he would have stuck it there, if possible, with glue.

He felt very relieved. It was the kind of relief one felt upon coming back home from walking in the scorching sun. What would that tired man do first, upon reaching home? He would go to the well, draw a bucketful of cold water, wash his hands and feet, drink a glassful of kanjivellam and stretch his limbs in an armchair. If there was a fan, he would switch it on. That's exactly what Kesavan did. After writing down the title, he put his pen down on the table, walked over to the well, washed his face in the cold water, drank a glass of kanjivellam with some salt and stretched himself out in the armchair. The leaves of the hibiscus bush were gently swaying in the midday breeze. Kesavan lay there with eyes closed.

But the quietude of his mind didn't last long. Unwittingly, a conflict was slowly developing in his mind. Appukkuttan's story was not even halfway through. To push it forward, he had yet to write another 100, perhaps 150 pages. Anywhere between 25,000 to 35,000 words… He experienced, in advance, the pressure of those yet-to-be written words. The anxiety over whether he could discard the evasive words and symbols he is looking for, caused him immense strain. The veins in his head were swollen and his temples throbbed. Writing induces high blood pressure in him. When he sits down to write, his bp rises to 160/100. He was sure it would certainly be much more if he measured the pressure just then. He lay in the armchair closing his eyes to calm the rising bp.

Ravunni, Pavithran and Unni Kurup came in through the gate. Kesavan had no inclination to see anyone or to sit around talking at that moment. He felt like jumping up from the chair and hiding under the cot or behind the almirah, but before he could do anything, the trio had already reached the courtyard. Kesavan lay as if in some yogic exercise of rest.

'Is the 'world-famous writer' in meditation?' Ravunni said.

'Like we say, 'Moha Nidra,' can't we say 'Sarga Nidra'? This is Kesavan's Sarga Nidra,' said Unni Kurup.

'Sarga Nidra is a term that suits one well, though. It's not from the conscious mind but from sleep in which he catches hold of ideas to write about.'

Ravunni stepped into the house holding up one end of his mundu. He was wearing a silk khadi kurta. His frequent Delhi tours bring about this kind of change in his sartorial appearance. It was a white Lucknowi kurta that he had been wearing when he returned from his latest trip to Delhi.

Pavithran and Unni Kurup were with Ravunni. Ravunni never visits them alone. On his trip from Kozhikode he picks up both of them. If he fails to get both, he will angle for at least one of them.

'Kesavan! Don't sulk now. I haven't come to pester you. It is to give you some good news that I've come, spending 500 rupees on the taxi fare. I'll leave right after giving you the news.'

Ravunni sat down near Kesavan. He reeked of brandy.

'Now, you'll be able to fly to Delhi once in a while. And stay in Kerala House or India International Centre, go about sight-seeing... I have arranged your nomination to the Akademi. That's the first bit of good news.'

'Don't you know that I am not interested in such things?'

'But I am. That's why I got it done, falling at the Chief Minister's feet, so to say.'

'Why did you do it without even asking me? To discredit me before the Chief Minister?'

'It's not you—it's I who fell at the CM's feet. If there is some discredit to anyone, it's to me, not to you.'

'But I'm not willing to accept it.'

'Kesavan! Your arrogance is crossing all limits.'

'I don't need any office or position. I am saying this not to play goody-goody in front of others. Only that I am not interested. That's all.'

'Don't take any decision in a hurry. Think it over,' Ravunni said, unperturbed. After that he peered into the interior of the house and called out:

'Sujatha! What are you doing inside? Have you too begun playing hide-and-seek like Kesavan?'

'I'm right here.'

'Then bring three glasses.'

Sujatha washed three glasses, wiped them clean and brought them over. Along with water, in a pitcher. Cool water drawn from the well just then.

'You haven't yet told him the second bit of good news,' Pavithran reminded Ravunni.

'I'm not going to reveal it for the time being. He's not interested in anything.'

'At whose feet have you fallen this time, for my sake?'

Ravunni refused to divulge anything more on the subject. He felt indignant. He swore to himself that he would never do anything for Kesavan anymore. Kesavan, the ingrate.

Taking out the bottle from the bag, Ravunni poured an equal measure in all three glasses. Unni Kurup added water.

Kesavan watched as brandy and water mixed in the glasses.

Ravunni had given up the habit of carrying his shoulder bag for quite some time. The reason was that he had stopped drinking. Now, the bag has reappeared on his shoulder. But certain changes have begun to appear in him. Now he doesn't drink in public places like bars or restaurants. And he is becoming slightly plump. Now he wears a clean mundu and shirt. And has dispensed with bus travel altogether.

'Hey! Where has your novel reached?'

Pavithran enquired. The corners of his moustache were wet with the brandy.

Kesavan didn't say anything.

'Ravunni Master! It is useless coming over here and meeting Kesavan like this. He sees us as his enemies. He has nothing to tell us. Isn't he always looking at us with suspicion? Are we thieves? Have we come here to abduct his wife?' Pavithran continued, with rising indignation.

'Kesavan always pulls a fast one on us. Never tells us anything openly. Has Kesavan ever opened his heart to us? Or treated us like his buddies? And told us a single thing about him?'

'Hey, Pavithran! Don't flare up. Kesavan is like this. What can we do about it?' said Ravunni. 'Kesavan, to me, is what he writes. There is no element of artifice in his writing. His books speak to me like a child. That's enough for me. If deceit so much as touches the words he writes, if those words lie to me, I'll never again set foot in this house again.'

Kesavan, sitting in his chair, didn't respond even to that.

'Don't you want anything to munch?' Sujatha appeared at the doorway.

'What do you have?'

'There's mixture. And some rice flakes.'

'Bring the rice flakes. Don't keep that spicy salty mixture in your house—it raises one's BP. Don't give Kesavan even a little of that, Sujatha,' Ravunni went on. 'Sujatha, I've been troubling you for a long time now. I come in at odd hours and I make you cook rice or make tea for me. From now on, you can take rest. Our Pavithran is going to get married.'

'Who said you're troubling me, Ravunni Master? You are always welcome,' said Sujatha. 'Pavithran, where's your girl from?'

'Near-by. From Chalappuram.'

'This Pavithran had sworn never to get married. He had boasted that he'd live with a girl without marrying her. And now, look at him—he's getting married, like everybody else,' Unni Kurup said and licked the edges of his brandy-soaked moustache.

Eating the rice flakes mixed with grated coconut and washing it down with brandy, they carried on their conversation. As usual, Kesavan remained a mere listener between the exchanges took place between Unni Kurup and Pavithran. Kurup is a confirmed bachelor. He resented Pavithran's decision to marry. From the day his marriage had been fixed, Kurup began quarrelling with him.

When the bottle was finally empty, Ravunni said:

'Let's go now. Let Kesavan continue his meditation.'

Ravunni got up and slung the bag across his shoulder. The bag looked like the distended belly of a woman after her first pregnancy. When Pavithran dropped a lighted match in the empty bottle, blue flames leapt up inside with a 'whoosh' and then escaped the bottle, turning into smoke.

Kesavan got up from his chair and went out with them. The car was parked on the roadside. Autorickshaws pass through the by-lane, wide enough only for a cow to amble along. But cars cannot. One has to walk up to the road. Losing his balance, Ravunni held on to Unni Kurup's shoulder for support and walked forward.

'Hey, Kesavan! Didn't we say there was more good news? Listen now. You are going to get a telephone connection. I have done the necessary things. I have filled up the application form on your behalf, forging your signature. And I have deposited the money as well. And there will be a phone connection in your house within a week. Okay?'

'Why does this one who doesn't talk to anyone need a phone?' said Pavithran. 'Ravunni Master, please arrange to have that connection shifted to my house. Am I not getting married?'

They all got into the car. As the engine revved up and the car began to move, Kesavan touched Ravunni's fat hand softly, once.

The car reversed and raced away towards Kozhikode, spewing black smoke. Unni Kurup and Pavithran would get down at the Fifth Railway Gate. Just dropping in once at home in Koyilandi en route, Ravunni would continue his journey towards Kozhikode.

Sixteen

After seeing off Ravunni and company, Kesavan came back to his room and closed the door. After about half of *Appukuttan's Lamentations* was finished, a new character had popped up. The arrival of a new character, even as the other characters of the novel continued pestering him, hardly pleased Kesavan. He always experiences his characters as living entities. All of them have their own sorrows, dreams, joys, hunger, thirst, love, lust, envy and hatred. Kesavan's characters crowd around him; never once leaving him wherever he goes, they follow him like shadows. When he goes to his office, jostled about in a bus, they too push in after him. When he lies down in bed with Sujatha, they too share the bed.

He read the last written line in the novel:

Appukkuttan, Vasudevan and Padmavathy are walking to school. The sky, bearing the welts of rain-clouds, hangs low like a pandal propped up on bamboo poles. The poles may break, and the sky collapse, at any moment. Vasudevan, who was scared of the rain, walked fast. Padmavathy's hair and powdered face were oily.

'Your head and face look wet. Did you get wet in the rain?'

'That's because Mother gave me a oil bath.'

'Is it your mother who bathes you?'

'Who else bathes children?'

'Do you bathe without any clothes on?'

'Umm...'

'Aren't you ashamed?'

'I'm only a child...'

Yet, Padmavathy's oily cheeks turned ruddy...

Kesavan sat staring at the newspaper.

Why did I insert such a scene, mused Kesavan. For whom did I compose these lines? Kesavan had never intended to create such an episode. Yet, how were those lines born from his pen?

Appukkuttan is growing up, Kesavan realised. The natural curiosities of a growing boy might be awakening in him as well. Just because Appukkuttan is a character created by him, he cannot keep away from taking charge of not only his family life and social life, but sex life as well, Kesavan realised. He became aware that he could not shirk that responsibility.

He put down the pen he had picked up to strike out the paragraph.

He also recalled what Ravunni once said: 'You can't ignore the sexuality of your characters. If you do, it will be in bad taste.'

It was Ravunni, the father of four children, who gave Kesavan that lesson.

The realisation that he could not in any way escape from the responsibility of Appukkuttan's sexuality caused another kind of conflict in Kesavan. That inner conflict grew and alarmed him. Kesavan's notion that he was merely writing the story of a child who worshipped EMS, and about the problems that that devotion raised around him, was being challenged. Thus, Kesavan became convinced that whether he liked it or not, different aspects of Appukkuttan's sexuality were going to be unleashed in the novel.

Kesavan, who never wished to write about sex, sat harbouring a feeling of suffocation.

It was with the casualness of that small conversation between Appukkuttan and Padmavathy that the new character called Aaman came in. Such a character had never existed in Kesavan's mind. Yet, on a cold dawn, when he sat down to write after the cozy warmth of a cup of tea, he saw that strange character in front of him. Had Aaman jumped in through the window from outside!

'Who are you?'

'Aaman. A poor migrant.'

'With whose permission did you migrate into this novel?'

Aaman let down his hitched-up mundu without saying a word.

'This is not immigration, but transgression.'

Kesavan felt that Aaman was not a character to be subdued easily, going by his rigid face muscles and hard stare.

'What's your name?'

'Aaman Master.'

'Everyone around here is some kind of master. Postmaster, tuition master and some call even *me* 'Master.' What kind of a 'Master' are you?'

'An unemployed Master. I am wandering about without a job after completing Teacher Training.'

Kesavan didn't miss the humour of the situation. His neighbour Aravindan, too, was unemployed. Whenever he learned that a top leader or officer was visiting Kesavan, he would prowl around Kesavan's house like a cat and entreat him to speak to them about finding a job for him. Now, here was another one coming to him, begging for a job.

There is, however, one difference between Aravindan and Aaman. Aravindan came to him, prowling around. This man, instead, came jumping in through the window, hitching up his mundu. Aaman was a daredevil and an aggressor. Kesavan felt that if he didn't handle him properly, he would plant rubber all through his novel. And sell the latex and make money. Isn't he a migrant from the south, like Thomaskunju?

'Sir, please sit down.'

'Are you making fun of me?'

'No. There are more than enough "masters" here. Only "sirs" are missing.'

Aaman Sir sat down. His shoulders were extraordinarily broad.

'I am being frank, Aaman Sir. Please do not think ill of me. If I try on your behalf, no one will give you even a scavenger's job, let alone a teacher's. I am just a poor writer.'

Derisive laughter crinkled Aaman's eyes. In the discomfiture brought about by that laughter, Kesavan stood cowed like a capitalist unwittingly trapped inside the CITU office.

After a while, Kesavan continued, mustering all his courage.

'A writer cannot accomplish a thing. When we writers appear in public, people come and get our autographs. And the snobs among them will take photos, posing with us. When we deliver a speech, TV crews will be there, covering our programmes. All this is true. But who attaches any value to our words? Who will listen to our recommendations? Therefore, sir, please go and meet our MP, Mr Kumaran. He will be at home, since the Parliament is not currently in session. Tell him that I sent you. Now, you may go, Sir, please. I have work to do. Though I'd like to give you some tea, there is no milk in the house. Besides Sujatha is fast asleep, Once I woke her from sleep and asked her to make tea. She fumbled about drowsily, made some tea and brought it to me. She had added salt to the tea, instead of sugar, in her stupor. I don't at all wish to give you salty tea first thing in the morning, sir. Before the MP leaves his house, please go, meet him and tell him about your need. If you want, I'll give you a letter introducing you to the MP.'

Aaman Sir laughed. This time it was not with his eyes, but with an open mouth. Aaman Sir took out a paper folded into four from his pocket and handed it to him without any comment. Kesavan's hand trembled as if he was accepting a love-letter. It was a letter from Kumaran. Kesavan held it out in the light and read:

'The bearer of this letter is someone very close to me. He has completed teacher training. I know that you are in touch with several people in high places. Kindly place this young man somewhere.'

'All right,' said Kesavan. 'Let me try and contact the manager of the school where Appukkuttan is studying.'

'I'll never forget this kindness.'

Aaman Sir bowed his head in obeisance.

Dawn broke outside. Crows were cawing. He saw Moosath bobbing along the lane. Visalakshi Ezhuthamma's head was not to be seen.

Aravindan, who was standing on the embankment, came down and moved close to Kesavan quietly.

'Kesavetta, I am tired of life. I feel like killing myself.'

'The day hasn't dawned yet. Do you plan to die before that?'

'There is no dawn in the life of people like me, Kesavetta; there is only night.'

'Good. So you can sleep to your fill.'

'If you make up your mind, you can find a job for me. I know it. It's because you don't try. I am ready to work even as a peon. I cannot go about without a job any more. Who else can I tell my woes to, but you Kesavetta?'

'I don't have the time to listen to others' woes now. Till now, you took me for an Employment Exchange and came to me every day saying you wanted a job. And you have begun telling me your woes too, have you? Am I the Sai Baba, to listen to others' woes? You must not be seen in front of me anymore. Seeing your face first thing in the morning will ruin my day. Don't ruin my mood now; go on, get out…

Keshavan shooed away Aravindan from there as if he were a dog.

Aravindan walked away, crestfallen. Without going back home, he again went over to the embankment and began counting the heads of the passersby.

Seventeen

Appukkuttan had failed in the examinations once again.

Vasudevan, his classmate, passed and overtook him. And Padmavathy, who was a class below, arrived alongside him. She felt very happy about it. Because, now she could sit in Appukkuttan's class, next to him, on the same bench....

She is determined to marry Appukkuttan when he grows up. She, who is to share his bed in future, can at least share his bench now.

Ananthakrishnan was saddened by his son's failure. He doesn't aspire to send him to professional colleges, to make him a doctor or an engineer. Just push him along somehow and see him through a BA—that's his only goal.

Another person who was troubled over Appukkuttan's failure was Aaman Sir. He knows that the reason for his failure was not any lack of intelligence. He has observed that Appukkuttan is much more intelligent than many other pupils. The relation between intelligence and passing examinations is a subject he is fascinated by. Is intelligence really necessary to pass examinations? How is it that certain pupils who are unintelligent score high marks in examinations?

Aaman Sir decided to study this subject. The main compulsion he felt in carrying out this study was Appukkuttan's failure. He began to watch Appukkuttan's movements. He paid special attention to things Appukkuttan did and said. He was very keen to find out what thoughts were passing through Appukkuttan's mind.

Aaman Sir, who hailed from a faraway region, did not know anything about Appukkuttan's circumstances or his past.

It was The Two Drunks who opened up Appukkuttan's past in front of Aaman Sir one day. The Two Drunks rarely sat on the culvert after they had been defeated in the battle with Saravanan. At the mere sight of Saravanan in the distance, they'd flee.

'Give us ten rupees. We haven't slaked our throats since morning,' The Two Drunks said, seeing Aaman Sir approaching.

'Are you the two drunks of this area?' asked Aaman Sir.

'Which other area can you visualise us in? We were born and brought up here. And we will die upon this soil,' The Two Drunks affirmed.

'Do you know Appukkuttan's father, Ananthakrishnan?'

'Give us ten rupees; then we'll tell you.'

Aaman Sir took out ten rupees and gave it to The Two Drunks. Aaman Sir, who was a Marxist, adopted the classic method of the KGB to extract secrets.

Drunk Number One: 'Ananthakrishnan was a Naxalite. But he shits in his pants in fear.'

Drunk Number Two: 'Appukkuttan's mother is dead.'

Aaman Sir: 'How did she die at such a tender age? Who brought up the motherless Appukkuttan?'

The Two Drunks: 'We'll tell you the rest tomorrow. We're off now.'

They had seen Saravanan approaching; they rose from the culvert and fled.

Saravanan came along, swaying on unsteady legs and sat down on the culvert. Saravanan's body is as slight as a coconut leaf midrib, and he has spindly legs thinner than his hands. His legs seem to have been fitted where his hands should have been and vice versa. He has begun to realise that the world is a place where everything is functioning from the wrong places. He believes that even man's intelligence is situated in the wrong place.

'Aren't those The Two Drunks that left just now?'

'Yes. Who are you? The Third Drunk?'

'I'll tell you if you give me five rupees.'

One of the main expenses Aaman Sir incurs after coming to this place, has been doling out money to The Two Drunks. Aaman Sir, who does not drink, likes drunks. Because, they always speak the truth. Not a single drunk has ever lied to him. He was sure that what The Two Drunks told him about Ananthakrishnan would also be the truth.

'Do you know Appukkuttan father Ananthakrishnan?'

'Give me five rupees and I'll tell you.'

'I have only this much now,' Aaman Sir took out the three rupees remaining and gave it to Saravanan.

'Was Ananthakrishnan a Naxalite?'

'Umm. But he shits in his pants with fear.'

Aaman Sir was confused for a moment as to whether Saravanan or The Two Drunks had said that. It may be that all drunks spoke in the same way. The direct language of truth.

'Isn't Appukkuttan's mother alive?'

'She died in childbirth.'

Aaman Sir felt that there was nothing more to be asked of him just then. The information that The Two Drunks gave him about Appukkuttan's parents were confirmed by Saravanan.

Father: Ex-Naxalite.

Mother: Died in childbirth when he was still a small boy.

Aaman Sir felt that it was but natural if Appukkuttan was different from other children of his age. He now has a key with which to unlock Appukkuttan's doors.

'Who're you?'

'Appukkuttan's Master at the school.'

Aaman Sir walked towards the school without further comment. Children were entering the school in droves. Along with them came Appukkuttan, Vasudevan and Padmavathy. Appukkuttan had rolled up his shirtsleeves above the elbows. As if in permanent preparation to face his opponents.

'Comrade, please stop. Let me ask you something.' Saravanan, sitting on the culvert with his dirty mundu folded up above his thighs, said.

'Don't stop. Let's move on...,' Padmavathy told Appukkuttan, lowering her voice.

'Is what I heard true? That you failed in the examinations once again?'

Padmavathy tried to pull Appukkuttan away from the scene. She always felt repulsed when she saw Saravanan. She was afraid of him, too. Whenever she spotted him from a distance, her heart skipped a beat.

'What is it to you if I have failed? Who are you to ask this question? My father?'

'So what I heard is true. Don't worry, Appootta. Go and join the Marxist Party. It's a party of the exam-failed.'

Stroking his straggling arrack-drenched beard Saravanan smiled a yellow smile, looking at Appukkuttan.

'I'll have you picked up by the police.'

'I've seen enough of police and the military. Ask your father. He'll tell you.'

'Come, Appootta...'

Padmavathy began to run, dragging him along. While running thus towards the school, he resolved that he would become a policeman when he grew up. On his very first day as a policeman, he would pick up a lathi, go out and arrest Saravanan. He turned around and glared at Saravanan.

By the time Appukkuttan had had a wash after he returned from school at noon and put away the satchel, Ananthakrishnan had served him rice in a plate. He had also prepared fish curry and lentils. He silently watched his son eating lunch. It was not with a father's eyes that Ananthakrishan watched his son then, but with a mother's. Much more than himself, it was Sreedevi who was within him whenever he ladled out rice and curry for Appukkuttan and fed him.

It was without any sense of order or neatness that Appukkuttan ate his lunch. Rice slipped through the gaps between his fingers. Each time he ladled out lentils from the bowl into his plate, half of them spilt over and fell on the table. Fish-bones were scattered over the table and on the ground. The cat and the cock that waited outside for them, rushed in as soon as Appukkuttan rose from the table.

Aaman Sir came over to Appukkuttan's house in the evening. Everyone has certain peculiarities. Aaman sir's is that he has extraordinarily broad shoulders and a thin waist. His mundu would never be firmly wound around his waist. That gives him many troubles. Especially when he travels in buses. He even plans to wear a belt around his mundu like Sooppy Mappila. He had once seen the students' union leader Lakshmanan brandishing his belt against an opponent in front of the college. He saw the opponent Vidyadharan's ears bleeding and eyes popping from the belt-lashes delivered by Lakshmanan. Lakshmanan wore a belt not to prevent his mundu from falling down, but to thrash his opponents. Although it was an incident that had happened way back in the past, Aaman Sir would remember Lakshmanan whenever he saw a belt.

'We don't know each other. I'm Appoottan's Master, Aaman Sir....'

'I know who you are. I was planning to come over to meet you. To tell you about Appu. I am losing my peace of mind, Thinking about him, Sir. Please, do sit down....'

Aaman Sir, who was holding fast onto his mundu by the waist, sat down in a chair. It was a large chair. He felt as if he had landed in a pit, buttocks first. For a person like him with a slim waist, that broad-seated chair was an extravagance. Yet, he sat on it.

'Sir, in the remote past, I had desires and dreams about so many things. Now, there are none. Cooking and eating, my days roll by. I don't have any great expectations about Appu. Still, shouldn't he pass at least BA? Shouldn't he get at least a clerk's job? Or else, how is he going to live after I am gone? But how is he going to reach college if he is failing in every class like this? That's my great worry now...'

'Please don't worry. Appoottan has some problem. He'll be all right once the problem is identified and addressed. Appoottan is a very intelligent child. I came to learn more about him....'

Ananthakrishnan was a little put off hearing this. Has Aaman Sir come to sound him out about his own past, he wondered. Ananthakrishnan doesn't want to remember any of it. He prayed that Aaman Sir would not urge him to open the moth-eaten baggage of the memories of yesteryears.

'Where does Appoottan sit and study?'

'He doesn't have any one specific place to sit for study. Sometimes he even sits in the kitchen and studies.'

'Does he do his homework all by himself? Don't you help him with it?'

'Where's the time for that? I have to wash the clothes, cook rice and curry. Sweep the house and the yard...'

He spends a major portion of the day in the kitchen. It keeps him from moving away from life.

'Where are Appoottan's books kept?'

'There...'

Ananthakrishnan pointed towards one side of the room. Appukkuttan's satchel was lying on a big table close to the wall.

Besides the satchel there was an iron box, a kerosene lamp, glasses and a tin. Oil and tea stains stuck fast to the table.

At another end of the table, clothes were folded and piled up. A sigh escaped Aaman Sir, as he looked around.

'You must set apart a particular space for Appoottan's study. Tell him to sit at this place to study. That office room is best suited. As soon as he comes back from school, he must put his books there.'

Aaman Sir spoke to Ananthakrishnan as if he was talking to Appukkuttan. What Appukkuttan needs is order and neatness. He clearly identified in that house, the daily chaos in the life of a husband without a wife and a child without a mother.

Ananthakrishnan and Aaman Sir sat talking about many things for a while. Fortunately, Aaman Sir didn't inquire into Ananthakrishnan's past. Ananthakrishnan feared that that would happen anytime now.

The new generation may not know everything about his past. Earlier some journalists used to come in search of him from time to time. They were feature writers. He would speak to them about the stench of the ration rice he got from fair price shops, the soaring prices of vegetables, the shortage of drinking water owing to the late arrival of rains, the incident of the burglar breaking into Sooppy Mappila's house and a cat falling into Moosath's well. The feature writers, who realised that they would not get from his mouth anything about the topic they were after, would leave, yawning and dejected. In fact, none of them returned a second time.

As far as Ananthakrishnan is concerned, his past is a box that is carefully closed and sealed. It is not easy to prise it open. It may not be possible anymore for him to clearly pronounce words like dialectical materialism, class war, petit-bourgeois and so on.

'Don't you worry,' Aaman Sir consoled Ananthakrishnan as he was leaving. 'Appoottan will be all right. I'll make him all right.'

Aaman Sir took Ananthakrishnan's hand and shook it. His hand had turned rough with grinding and pounding in preparation for cooking, and washing clothes.

I can understand the Ananthakrishnan who sought refuge in the kitchen after giving up guerilla warfare, Aaman Sir said to himself, as he was walking along the streets all alone. I can't understand why he has kept a framed picture of EMS, though. That created confusion in his otherwise lucid mind. At the same time, he was inwardly thrilled. Aaman Sir is an active worker of the Marxist Party. In his house too, there is a picture almost like that one. In that picture, painted by an anonymous artist, Comrade P. Krishna Pillai occupies the central, prominent position. And in the insets on the left and on the right respectively, AKG and EMS are portrayed.

Eighteen

For the first time in her life, Padmavathy had an enemy. It was Aaman Sir. His posture—smoking a cigarette, his walk—shrugging his shoulders, and his laughter twinkling his eyes, are far beyond her endurance. It is his stare that she can't at all put up with. Looking at his face, one got the impression that he was always just about to laugh at you.

Padmavathy's tender mind, that had never admitted hatred even for robbers, was now filled with repugnance for Aaman Sir.

She used to go to school every day together with Vasudevan and Appukkuttan. Those trips to the school and back were the best moments of her life. She wouldn't feel afraid even if they faced an elephant, when she was with them. They inspired such confidence in her. It was during the rainy season that she enjoyed those trips most. She and Vasudevan had only one umbrella between them. If she walked with Vasudevan under his umbrella, it was as good as having a shower with her clothes on. Therefore she walked under Appukkuttan's umbrella. A peculiar scent arose when Appukkuttan's new umbrella's canvas got wet in the rain. She enjoyed that smell very much.

But Aaman Sir had wrenched away that enjoyment from her...

'Appootta, stop.'

Aaman Sir, who had got off the bus, came towards them.

'I'll also come along with you children, what?'

Appukkuttan's face brightened. He hurriedly walked towards the Master. They stopped at the roadside and began to talk.

As Padmavathy stood perplexed, not knowing what to do next, Vasudevan caught her hand and pulled her along saying, 'Come along, girl.'

Till they reached the school, Padmavathy kept looking back over her shoulder. Aaman Sir and Appukkuttan were walking very slowly. When he walked, his shoulders were shaking as if a central screw of his body had gone loose. Her neck ached from constantly turning around.

The next day too, on their way to school, Aaman Sir was standing at the bus stop.

'Appootta, don't go away,' he said. 'Let me buy a cigarette.'

That day Padmavathy didn't turn around even once. Still her neck ached. Was it a memory of the previous day's pain?

It became a routine after that. Getting off the bus, Aaman Sir would wait for Appukkuttan.

During the games period, she secretly told Appukkuttan: 'Wait and see, Appoottan. The cow will gore Aaman Sir. I've prayed to Muttappan for that.'

'You cruel girl,' said Appukkuttan.

'I'll kill myself,' she sobbed.

In the obituary columns of *Mathrubhoomi*, the photo of a school student who had hanged herself had appeared once.

A girl a couple of years senior to Padmavathy. Padmavathy had seen her mother putting down the paper and whispering something to her father. My photo will be in that girl's place, she said to herself. Only then will Appukkuttan learn a lesson.

Padmavathy's rage didn't unsettle Appukkuttan. Much more than going to school with her, he liked to walk beside Aaman Sir. He learned that Aaman Sir knew EMS closely. Aaman Sir knew EMS's age and the name of the school where EMS had studied. Aaman Sir narrated many anecdotes concerning the life of EMS. If only he had been born as Aaman Sir's son, Appukkuttan wished.

'Have you seen Eeyyemmes, Sir?'

'At least a hundred times.'

'O my God...'Appukkuttan couldn't believe it.

'I too want to see him, once...'

'Certainly, why not?'

'Standing by the roadside, we can watch Eeyyemmes going to office.'

Aaman Sir laughed, 'Eeyyemmes doesn't go to office, Appootta.'

'Is he on leave?'

'Why should Eeyyemmes need an office or job? Where does Eeyyemmes have the time for all that? Working for the good of society is Eeyyemmes's job. To end exploitation. To eradicate poverty. That's Eeyyemmes's job.'

'Will Eeyyemmes get a salary for that?'

Aaman Sir laughed again, 'It's a job that doesn't pay a salary.'

Appukkuttan was aghast.

'You will understand everything pretty well, when you become bigger. When you grow up and become a big man.'

Appukkuttan yearned suddenly to grow up and become as tall as Moosath. Moosath was probably able to understand everything. Isn't he the tallest man in the area?

Appukkuttan's friendship with Aaman Sir pleased Ananthakrishnan no end. He felt that God had heard his plea. It was difficult for him to support Appukkuttan's burden all by himself. Because, he was not growing up like an ordinary child. Ananthakrishnan had realised that for an ordinary person like him, it would be difficult to take the sole responsibility for such a boy. Now he didn't have the capacity to respond to Appukkuttan's queries.

Appukkuttan was always full of eulogies of Aaman Sir. When Aaman Sir came home, he would talk only to Appukkuttan. As if he had nothing to tell Ananthakrishnan. Yes. What can he talk to Ananthakrishnan about?

Let this relationship of Appukkuttan with Aaman Sir help him pass the exams, prayed Ananthakrishnan. He must not fail henceforth. If he did, he may have to quit that school. That fear grew in him like a phobia. He made a vow that he would once again ascend the sacred Palani Hill, if Appukkuttan passed the exams. Let Appukkuttan be promoted somehow to the next class through the blessings of Palani Subrahmania Swamy. Is it Swamy Himself who sent Aaman Sir, for this purpose?

On a Sunday, Aaman Sir came to Ananthakrishnan's house, changing two buses en route. It was not usual for him to come on holidays. When he arrived, Ananthakrishnan was picking stones in the rice.

'I'll help you.'

'Oh, no, Sir!'

'I too know all these things, Ananthakrishnan. The first tea of the day I make myself. I wash my mundu and shirts myself. It's part of my principle not to depend on anyone for anything.'

Sitting beside Ananthakrishnan, he scanned the rice for stones. Since it was ration rice, there was enough for both of them to sit and pick.

'Where do you eat your lunch, sir? Do you go home for that?'

'Where is the time for all that? I have to change two buses to reach home.'

'Can't you rent a house somewhere near here, sir?'

'It is good to undergo a little suffering in life, like travelling in a crowded bus or going hungry during lunchtime.'

'Don't you eat anything during lunchtime?'

'No. Now it has become a habit. Now, even if I see rice and curry during lunch hour, I don't feel hungry.'

'This is not good, Sir. It's when you grow old that you suffer the evil effects of your not eating or sleeping when young. Sir, please come every day and eat your lunch from here.'

'No. I don't want to do that.'

Hearing their conversation, Appukkuttan came and stood on the doorstep. He didn't have a shirt on. His shorts had been fastened to his waist by a pin fixed at the waist-band.

'I'm going for a walk with Appoottan.'

No sooner did these words escape Aaman Sir's mouth, than Appukkuttan dashed in, put on a shirt, combed his hair and came back.

Watching Appukkuttan, Aaman Sir felt that there was some change in his appearance. Immediately he spotted it. Usually he combed his hair backwards. Today he had combed his hair parting it from left to right.

Like EMS.

'Your new hairstyle is nice.'

Aaman Sir wound his powerful hand around Appukkuttan's shoulder and walked on.

'You know the film star Dev Anand? There were people here in olden times who used to imitate his hairstyle. And there were girls who bobbed their hair in 'Sadhna' style. But you, Appukkuttan, are the first one to imitate the hairstyle of a communist leader.'

Appukkuttan was, for an instant, put off by the realisation that his closely guarded secret was out.

'There is a vast distance between film stars who run around trees, singing, and a leader of the proletariat. So stick with your new hairstyle.'

Whenever Appukuttan did something, Ananthakrishnan would oppose or criticise it. Vasudevan and Padmavathy behaved in the same way towards him. While everyone tried to find fault with him, it was Aaman Sir alone who approved of what he said or did.

Elated, Appukkuttan walked alongside Aaman Sir. When they reached the main road, they got into a bus. Since it was a Sunday, there was no rush of students. Aaman Sir and Appukkuttan got places to sit. But by the time they began to enjoy their seats, sitting, it was time for them to get down.

They had alighted at a small junction. There was a bus going to Kayanad, waiting there for passengers. Fisherwomen were sitting in front of small heaps of sardines and other fish, on one side of the road. The grains of sand that stuck to their dark legs, beneath their lungis, shimmered in the sun, occasionally. A row of shops also stood there. From the top of a roof, a red flag fluttered.

Aaman Sir crossed the road, holding Appukkuttan's hand.

'Isn't that Eeyyemmes's flag?' asked Appukkuttan, looking over his shoulder.

'Yes, the flag of the proletariat and the oppressed.'

They climbed a flight of steps sandwiched between a building where beedi workers sat in rows rolling beedis and a copra godown, and reached the second storey. A red flag was seen there too.

The flag tied to the pillar on the veranda hung limp, as there was no wind. Just as oxygen is necessary for human beings to breathe, wind is needed for flags to flutter. Aaman Sir led Appukkuttan to a room at the end of the verandah.

The almirahs lining the walls were full of books. There was a long table with two long benches on either side of it. Newspapers and magazines were scattered all over the table. The youngsters sitting on the benches looked up at them. Some of them greeted Aaman Sir. A couple of them stood up to show their respect to him.

'This is Appoottan. My student.'

An old man reading the newspaper removed his glasses and looked at him intently. It seemed that he had plastered his hair down with oil.

'Isn't this boy that Anantheshnan's son?'

'Yes, old man. But Appoottan is not like his father.'

'Who can be like Anantheshnan? Isn't he crazy?'

Had Appukkuttan heard the old man? Aaman Sir looked intently at Appukkuttan's face. Appukkuttan's attention was rivetted on the photos displayed on the walls. Except EMS, he could not identify any of them. Aaman Sir took him by the hand and led him to them.

'This is Comrade Krishna Pillai, this is AKG, this...'

'Eeyyemmes!'

'This is Comrade Azheekkodan Raghavan. This, Comrade C.H.Kanaran...'

'Who are they, Sir?'

'The high priests of revolution, who devoted their lives for the well-being of our land and its people. Comrade Krishna Pillai is the founder of the Communist movement here. He died of snakebite.'

Appukkuttan shuddered involuntarily.

A boy of Appukkuttan's age, in tattered clothes, brought two glasses of tea and put it down in front of them. His hands were covered with grime.

'Why does that boy wear torn clothes?'

'Because he is poor. Isn't he working in that teashop? That's why.'

Appukkuttan blew into the tea that Aaman Sir gave him as he drank it. Aaman Sir didn't drink the tea that was offered to him, and gave it to the old man instead. He lit a cigarette and exhaled the smoke. Most of the people sitting there reading the newspaper, were smoking. In the waist-fold of their lungis there were beedies and matchboxes.

Aaman Sir picked up a newspaper and held it up, showing it to Appukkuttan.

'This is *Desaabhimaani*. This is the paper of the starving millions. Which paper do you get at home?'

Appukkuttan couldn't find an immediate answer to that question. He had never seen a newspaper at home so far.

Appukkuttan leafed through *Desaabhimaani*. In it, he found photos of EMS in two places.

'May I take this paper?'

Pausing for a moment, Aaman Sir said, 'All right. Take it.'

He brought Appukkuttan back home in the evening. When they arrived, Ananthakrishnan was making wicks from an old mundu, for the lamp before the gods.

'I am entrusting my Appu to you, Sir. It is not enough if you teach him English and Maths, Sir. Teach him what life is. All that I have learned has gone wrong. Therefore, I can't teach anyone anything any more. Not even my son.'

Ananthakrishnan filled with coconut oil the lamp in which he had put the wicks, and lit it. The oil-soaked wicks crackled in the heat, smouldered and burst into full blaze. Ananthakrishnan stood in the fullness of dusk, with folded palms, his mind set on the gods.

Nineteen

Appukkuttan passed the examinations with high marks. He was ranked fourth in the class.

Ananthakrishnan couldn't believe it. Aaman Sir had performed a miracle.

Ananthakrishnan had employed every means at his disposal to prevent his son from failing that year as well. He had not only advised his son; he had scolded him and even threatened him with dire consequences. Once, even forgetting the fact that it was his son who stood in front of him, he had even fallen at Appukkuttan's feet in entreaty. And prayed to all the gods and pledged offerings. None of these yielded any result. Appukkuttan had failed then. While other children studied to pass exams, it seemed then that Appukkuttan studied to fail consistently.

He was certain that he would fail this time too and that he would be expelled from the school thereafter. If that happened, he would have to seek out a sub-standard, godforsaken school and fall at the feet of its authorities to get his son admitted there. He was mentally preparing himself for this. Wasn't he only nursing a modest wish of educating Appukkuttan up to BA? He didn't aspire, like the parents of other students, to see his son become a doctor or engineer, did he? But he really feared whether Appukkuttan would even get past class ten, let alone BA. It was then that Appukkuttan had passed, ranking fourth in the class.

'I'll never forget this, Sir.'

'What did I do?'

'Aaman saar, you saved my son's future.'

'When Appoottan grows up, he will save the future of all the people. He will become a great man.'

'No. Not that far...'

'Today Appoottan is merely our child. But when he grows up, he will become this land's own....'

'No...No...' Ananthakrishnan's voice was weary. He was hearing what he did not want to hear.

Not only Ananthakrishnan, everyone else began to say that it was Aaman Sir who was behind Appukkuttan's success. With that, the parents of children who were weak in their studies began to come in search of Aaman Sir. They pleaded with Aaman Sir to give tuitions to their children as well, and help them pass the exams. The affluent father of a dull child even invited Aaman Sir to stay in their house permanently. Aaman Sir aspired to become famous by serving people and making sacrifices for them. And yet his fame spread far and wide among the parents of dull children...

Aaman Sir looked in the mirror and smiled, winking. When he tired of seeing others' smiles, he would go and stand in front of the mirror to see his own. For him, the mirror is not just for observing oneself while combing hair, putting on the bindi.

applying collyrium on the eye rims or shaving, but also for observing one's own smile. Thus, Aaman Sir added another dimension to the meaning of a mirror.

Isn't Aaman Sir the one who gave Appukkuttan's life a new meaning?

It was by means of a small trick that he had achieved this.

Aaman Sir accompanied Appukkuttan to his class on the day the exams started. Seeing that the other students spoke among themselves in hushed tones, Padmavathy turned her face away. Appukkuttan's repeated failures were a topic of discussion among the students. They too believed, like Ananthakrishnan, that he would fail this time as well.

'Do you remember what I told you, Appootta?'

'Yes.'

'Wish you all the best!' Patting him on the shoulder, Aaman Sir sent him to the classroom.

Among the children waiting for the question paper, silence and anxiety grew. But in Appukkuttan, there was no trace of any conflict. When the class teacher walked into the class with question papers, many children looked as if they would burst into tears. Anxiety and fear were writ large on the faces of students who used to score the highest marks in the class. If Appukkuttan, who was used to failure, failed once more, it was hardly going to be news. The class teacher had written him off. She had already hinted to Ananthakrishnan that he had better seek admission for Appukkuttan in some other school.

When he got the question paper, Appukkuttan, instead of going through it, closed his eyes and sat still for a moment. In that meditation, EMS's face floated up vividly. Hair combed to one side, spectacles with thick frames, half-sleeved coarse white shirt. That meditation gave him confidence...

Opening his eyes, he looked at the question paper and began to write his answers calmly...

He wrote the exams in this manner every day. That's how he passed the exams, ranking fourth in the class.

With that, Aaman Sir became a virtual member of Ananthakrishnan's family. He went over there even at midnight sometimes. Once he slept there overnight and went to school along with Appukkuttan.

Padmavathy didn't talk to Appukkuttan at all anymore. If she happened to encounter him at school, she would either take another route or turn her face away.

'I am going to Kannur in the evening. Appukkuttan says he hasn't seen Kannur as yet. Shall I take him along?' Aaman Sir walked in hurriedly one day, and asked Ananthakrishnan. He was wearing a white shirt that reached down to his knees. Rolled-up sleeves. In his pocket, there was a packet of Scissors cigarettes.

'It's up to you, Sir.'

'It may be a little late when we come back. Don't panic.'

'When you are with him, Sir, why should I be afraid?'

Appukkuttan had been yearning for sometime now to go to Kannur. Padmavathy had gone up to Mangalapuram. It was she who had told him that Mangalapuram was beyond Kannur. Ananthakrishnan never took Appukkuttan anywhere. Once a year, they would go to Parassinikkadavu Mathappura to see Muttappan's Vellattu. That was the only journey they ever undertook. He had only a faint memory of going to Palani along with his father, both of them wearing ochre. As they ascended the steps up the hill, they had seen several monkeys that snatched away puffed rice and plantains from the hands of the pilgrims. Some of the monkeys had buttocks as red as hibiscus flowers. Those were his memories of that trip.

Kannur and Kozhikode were still the last frontiers of the earth for him. Appukkuttan decided that he would travel far and wide to many lands once he was grown up. He was also sure that it would not be with his father wearing ochre.

'How do we go?'

'We'll catch a bus from the junction.'

'What time will we reach Kannur?'

'It will take almost two hours. We have to change buses from Thalassery. If we get seats, it'll be fine, we can sit together talking about this and that. It is good to travel in trains and buses. It is so enjoyable sitting in the midst of the people. We should always be in the midst of the people. This is something you must always remember when you grow up. Never live away from the people.'

Except the Fast Passengers, all other buses passing through Appukkuttan's locality would stop at the Junction. When he saw the Fast Passenger to Payyannur speeding away, he felt like clapping. Appukkuttan liked to travel in buses that speed away.

'Why doesn't that Fast Passenger stop at the junction?'

'It has limited stops. It won't stop at every bus stop. It stops only at important centres like Thalassery and Kannur. The Fast Passenger is meant for long-distance travellers. We need to take only a Town Bus. We'll get down at Thalassery and catch some other bus.'

'We must catch a Fast Passenger from there.'

'Let's see. Let's first reach Thalassery.'

'Have you travelled in a train, Sir?'

'Yes. And you, Appukkuttan?'

'Yes, I have, too. When I went to Palani along with my father.'

'I don't understand many things your father says and does, Appootta.'

'Neither do I. Father speaks ever so softly. I tell Father to speak up at least when he talks to you, Sir.'

Aaman Sir laughed. Appukkuttan didn't understand why he laughed like that.

They reached the junction and stood there waiting for the bus. A van flying a red flag passed by. It was crammed with people. The people in the van thrust their fists in the air and raised slogans at those who were waiting for the bus. Appukkuttan didn't catch what they were shouting at the top of their voices. But he recognised the red flag that was tied to the bonnet of the van. 'Our flag!' he cried.

While waiting for the bus, Aaman Sir took out a cigarette, lit and puffed at it, sending up small clouds of smoke.

'At what age do people begin to smoke cigarettes?

'There is no age limit for that. Some begin while they are still at school. Don't you know our Kunhiraman Master, Appootta? He began smoking cigarettes only after retirement. Now he smokes one-and-a-half packets a day.'

'I'll also begin smoking when I reach class ten.'

'No. You begin only after your retirement, like Kunhiraman Master.' Aaman Sir looked at his disciple and laughed, winking.

He couldn't finish smoking the cigarette he had lit. The Town Bus to Thalassery had already arrived. He dropped the cigarette to the floor, stubbed it out, and got onto the bus, holding Appukkuttan's hand. There was no space in it even to set foot. With great difficulty, Aaman Sir squeezed Appukkuttan in between two fortunate ones who were seated.

'All are bound for Kannur,' Aaman Sir said, dropping his voice.

At Thalassery bus stand, the rush was more than usual. Vans, tempos and jeeps fluttering red flags, were parked here, there, everywhere. Alighting from the vehicles, the passengers gathered in front of the bunk shops that were doing brisk business selling sherbet, tea, cigarettes and beedis. Some of those who got out of cars bought sweet limes. When they peeled the lime, its sweet fragrance filled the air.

So much of rush at Thalassery for the meeting at Kannur! Then what would it be like in Kannur?

'Appootta, do you want something to drink? Sherbet or tea? We won't be able to get even a drop of water when we reach Kannur.'

Without waiting for Appukkuttan's reply, Aaman Sir bought him a sarsaparilla sherbet. Appukkuttan tried to catch the khus-khus that was floating on top of the sherbet with his tongue. Khus-khus is something that eludes capture. It slipped from the tongue. Aaman Sir didn't drink anything. As he continued to wait for the bus, he lit another cigarette and blew out the smoke. Because of his chain-smoking, his front teeth were stained.

After drinking tea, a group of youngsters got into a jeep and began to shout slogans.

'Let's go in a jeep.'

'Is there any place in it? For us, a bus would be better.'

'Why aren't red flags put up on buses?'

'One day the red flag will flutter from everywhere. O my Appootta, right now the red flag is flying in one third of the world.'

As usual, the bus arrived before he finished smoking the cigarette. He stubbed the cigarette against a telephone pole, dropped it to the ground and rushed towards the bus holding Appukkuttan's hand. People clung on to even the sides of the bus. In the rush, people pushed Appukkuttan forward and backward and crushed his toes underfoot. As the bus began to move, slogans boomed from all around. In that excitement, Appukkuttan forgot the pain in his feet. A slogan rose up to his throat and stopped there.

The bus lurched forward slowly. Several vehicles sporting red flags created countless traffic snags along the narrow roads. Red flags could be seen flying not only on top of vehicles and roofs, but even on treetops. The bus began to climb a slope, swaying and groaning. Beyond, a big procession was moving forward through the main street.

Climbing up and descending the slope, the bus ground to a halt.

'The bus cannot go forward any further. Everyone, please get down here.' The conductor called out.

On either side of the bus, crowds were surging forward like two rivers. Aaman Sir and Appukkuttan got out along with the others who shoved themselves out of the bus

'It's some distance to the maidan. Will you be able to walk?'

'Let's walk!'

He was so glad to walk. To walk as one among the flowing tide of people. It was the first time in his life he had seen such a crowd.

When they reached a junction, he saw processions converging at the intersection from all roads. Buses, jeeps and autos sporting red flags and festoons moved forward, mingling with the individual processions.

'Appootta, did you see that? That's a procession that's coming from Mavilayi. It was the place where Eeyyemmes lived underground in one Pokkan's hut. In 1940…'

From the direction Aaman Sir had pointed to, a procession of red flags was inundating the road.

'Do you know Appootta, the Madras Police had announced a reward of one hundred rupees for those who helped apprehend Eeyyemmes. Later they raised the amount to one thousand rupees. But would Pokkan hand him over to the police? Would a Communist betray his leader even if one thousand or one crore rupees is offered? No. A Communist can never become a Judas…'

'We must go to Mavilayi once.'

'We must go to Mavilayi, Kayyur, Punnapra, Vayalar and all the other places…'

It was dusk when they reached the junction. The sky had turned into one big, fluttering red flag. Hundreds of thousands of people had gathered there. Even then, the flow of many processions coming along different roads had not stopped. Red flags and people were moving like the currents of the deep sea.

'We'll know no defeat!
Not even at gun point!'

The slogans rising from the four directions echoed in Appukkuttan's ears. He felt as if his ears were ablaze.

'As long as the land of Kerala prevails
Eeyyemmes will reign over it!
Red Salute to Martyrs!
Long live the Revolution!'

Appukkuttan, who was standing there in the heat and the odour of the human ocean around him, shouted at the top of his voice: 'Long live Eeyyemmess!'

Suddenly the hundreds of thousands of people in the maidan began to turn around like a giant vortex...

'Appootta, look! There, Eeyyemmes...!!' Aaman Sir pointed. Far away, on the stage decorated by red flags and streamers, EMS rose like a red sun. As if the sun, which had already sunk in the western horizon, had come back the entire stage was imbued with a red light...

Twenty

Appootta... Eeyyemmes, the leader of the struggling and oppressed masses, was born in an aristocratic Namboodiri Brahmin family that traced back its ancestry to the lineage of the legendary Mezhattol Agnihotri. It was a family of aadhyas or aristocrats. You wouldn't now understand what aadhya or aasya means. Understand one thing. Eeyyemmes was born in one of the most illustrious families in the highest caste of our land.

There is a similarity between you and Eeyyemmes. You grew up without your mother. And Eeyyemmes, without his father. Eeyyemmes's father died when he was still a very small child. You don't remember your mother's face, do you? Likewise, Eeyyemmes doesn't remember his father's face.

Eeyyemmes is now an atheist. Which means that he is not one who believes in God. But in those times? There were two sanctums within the precincts of his home. Sreeraman and Durga were the deities worshipped there. When he was a small boy, Eeyyemmes would get up early in the morning, take a bath and enter the two sanctums to perform japa. And visit the two temples near their ancestral home to worship and collect prasad. As he belonged to an ancient family of Vedic Brahmins who specialised in the recital of the Vedas, he learned the Rig Veda well enough to chant it, from any point, while he was still very young. Eeyyemmes grew up doing japa, praying, learning the Vedas by rote and doing the yogic Surya Namaskara. The greatest wish of his mother, who loved her son more than her life, was to see him become a great Othan or an adept at the recital of the Vedas. That he should become famous by taking part in Kadavalloor Anyonyam, a great conclave of Vedic Brahmins where a contest in the recital of Vedas was held. And yet, when he grew up, he became a Communist leader...

Appootta, it's when we tread a different path than the one ordained by the gods that we become great men. Eeyyemmes was one such great man who chose his own path...

That was a time when the high-caste jenmis or zamindars and the rich classes lived like gods. The Namboodiris could do as they pleased. They could have three wives. And besides, maintain liaisons known as sambandham, with any number of women throughout the land. There were many in Eeyyemmes's family who had married thrice. All of them had as many women, and as much money and power as they liked. Was it a matter of good fortune to be born a Namboodiri? But our Eeyyemmes was a person who decided that he would have none of this good fortune. Is it a small thing to forfeit the Brahminhood one gets as a result of the punya one has done throughout several births, my dear Appootta?

Look at what Eeyyemmes has written about his own community (Aaman Sir takes out a note from his pocket and reads out):

> This community is that of gods on earth. It was them that Parasuraman had appointed as the owners of the landed properties and as lords of Kerala. Be at the apex of the caste system, exact a huge sum as lease rent, remain the best friends and confidants of the rulers of the land.... Through all these, this caste remains at the topmost position in society.

Appootta, those who had to suffer the worst due to the inequities in the Namboodiri community were their women and serfs. There were many women in the Namboodiri community who had to spend their entire lives without seeing their husbands, as these men had several other wives. And the lot of the serfs was even worse. Eeyyemmes grew up seeing and hearing all these. Eeyyemmes was barely your age then, Appootta.

It was then that Eeyyemmes joined Edakkunni Namboodiri Vidyalayam and began to learn English. The children of aadhya Namboodiri families were not supposed to join schools. They were supposed to learn only Vedic hymns. And yet, Eeyyemmes dared to learn English, which they had described as *Mleccha Bhasha* or the language of the aliens. The study of English helped Eeyyemmes to learn that there was a whole universe outside Brahminhood.

During those times when Namboodiri boys couldn't go to school, Eeyyemmes not only studied English, but joined college as well. It was in 1929 that Eeyyemmes joined St Thomas' College, Thrissur, for the Intermediate Course. Do you know what Eeyyemmes learnt there? History of India, Ancient History, Logic and the like. From then onwards, Eeyyemmes had become involved in social reformist activities. Eeyyemmes protested against the practice of men sporting a tuft on top of their heads. Many other young men joined Eeyyemmes. When Munthiringod Bhavatratan Namboodiripad was asleep in Yogakshemam Lodge in Thrissur, they cut away his tuft. It was an incident that created a lot of furore in those days. Do you know why Eeyyemmes and his companions did such a thing? I'll tell you. That tuft was the symbol of caste, corrupt practices and the arrogance of power. That's why they cut away Bhavatratan Namboodiripad's tuft of hair.

Eeyyemmes didn't study in Thrissur for long. He took part in a protest, a satyagraha during that time. And the police arrested all those who took part in the satyagraha.

When news reached his mother that Eeyyemmes was arrested by the police, it broke her heart. She loved Eeyyemmes more than her own life. There was an extraordinary bond between the two of them. The police had arrested her son, the male heir of Elamkulam Mana, and imprisoned him! Could there be a greater disgrace for her? It was not only the loss of family honour that struck her a paralysing blow. The fear that something terrible would happen to her son was equally benumbing. She had never before suffered so much pain in her life.

The police had taken Eeyyemmes straight to Kannur. When we went to Kannur once, didn't I show you the Central Jail, there, Appootta? That's a place where they lock up thieves and murderers. It was there that they locked up Eeyyemmes. (Appukkuttan's eyes filled with tears.)

The court sentenced Eeyyemmes to three years' imprisonment. After putting him in Kannur Jail for sometime, they shifted him to Vellore Jail. It was bigger than the Kannur Jail.

Great freedom fighters and revolutionaries had been imprisoned there. Eeyyemmes didn't waste his time in jail. He was reading all the time. It was in Vellore Jail that Eeyyemmes read about the Russian Revolution and thought deeply about it. There, Eeyyemmes wrote some books as well.

Eeyyemmes returned from jail after serving his term, and decided to enter full-time politics, engaging in revolutionary activities. Though Eeyyemmes's mother was opposed to this, she never stood against him. His mother had a great mind, Appootta.

The police trailed Eeyyemmes everywhere. They would come to his house anytime and check out his books and papers. Seeing all this, Eeyyemmes's mother was deeply wounded. She believed that some great misfortune was going to befall Eeyyemmes. She wasted away in that fear and pain. One day, Eeyyemmes's mother died leaving him for ever, leaving him alone hounded by the police...

But it was when his elder brothers didn't permit him to perform his mother's funeral rites that he was pained the most. Though he was a Brahmin, Eeyyemmes did not wear the sacred thread. Eeyyemmes had been declared an outcaste for taking part once in a widow remarriage. When his beloved mother's funeral was taking place, Eeyyemmes couldn't even go near the pyre. He had to witness it from a distance. What a pity, my dear Appootta...

The next year, that is, in 1937, two very important things happened in Eeyyemmes's life.

The first was that Eeyyemmes married. (Appukkuttan was abashed.)

She was a girl who didn't know how to read and write, who knew nothing about the world outside. Her name was Arya.

Do you want to hear what Eeyyemmes says about his marriage? 'When my sixty-year-old mother died, the sixteen-year-old Arya came to fill that void.' Arya showered on Eeyyemmes the same amount of love his mother had given him.

Appootta, our Eeyyemmes is a great man well-loved not only by his mother and wife, but by all the people as well.

Didn't I say two things happened? I'll now tell you the second incident.

It was in 1937 that the first Communist Group was formed in our land. And Eeyyemmes took a lot of trouble to accomplish that feat. The government banned the Communist Party. They began to suppress the Party and hunt down the Communists. To escape from the clutches of the police, Eeyyemmes went underground. If he had not done so, the police would have killed him. They detested Eeyyemmes so much. It was Eeyyemmes who organised labourers, small farmers and others as one entity. That was why they hated Eeyyemmes.

As you know now, it was in the hut of Pokkan of Cheru Mavilayi that Eeyyemmes hid. It was during his life in hiding there that Eeyyemmes thought, read and wrote. The Madras police could not catch Eeyyemmes, though they combed the entire land. They advertised in the papers that they would give a reward of one thousand rupees to anyone who helped apprehend Eeyyemmes. Pokkan and the people of Mavilayi didn't even have enough to eat. And yet they didn't betray Eeyyemmes. That's why I say, Appootta, that all people love Eeyyemmes.

The police, jenmis and the rich are bound to hate the Communists. But the poor will always love them.

To be born a Communist, live and die as one...O my Appootta, it's such great good fortune...

Twenty-two

Ananthakrishnan stormed down the stairs of the Party Office, clutching his son's hand. The wooden stairs groaned under his heavy steps. Even after reaching the street, having descended the last step of the staircase, he didn't let go of his son's hand. He seemed to fear that if he let his son go, he would run away somewhere that instant.

'So you haven't forgotten the Party Office, have you?' said Bhargavan who was standing there like the sentinel of the Party Office. He was the Area Secretary of the Party.

'I have seen the Party and the Red Flag much before you did, remember that.' Ananthakrishnan exploded. Hearing the commotion, the tailor Ramanan craned his neck from his shop and looked. The measuring tape was wound around his neck.

It was unusual to find Ananthakrishnan so angry or excited. His conduct was that of a sattvic, peaceful, calm person. His eyes and face are always tranquil. Even while working with extremists, his nature was so serene. Kunhikkannan Master used to say that it was because he could never be agitated that he would not make a good revolutionary.

'Why are you so angry? What did I say to merit this?'

'If you try to spoil my son, I'll set fire to your Party Office.'

'Who's trying to spoil your son? I don't understand what you say.'

'You wouldn't understand. You and your Partymen seem to have cataracts in your eyes.'

'If there's cataract in our eyes, let it remain there. What is it to you?'

People came down from the Party Office and from the copra godown. They all stood around Ananthakrishnan.

'Let go of my hand, Father. It hurts.'

Instead of letting go, Ananthakrishnan further tightened his grip on his son's hand. Appukkuttan had never thought that the hand that bathed him, that fed him rice and that stroked his head while he was sleeping could be so rough. His nails were as sharp as the teeth of the coconut grater. His fingers clamed at Appukkuttan's soft hand.

'Anantheshna, let go of your son's hand,' said Bhargavan. 'If you don't like it, let Appoottan not come here any more.'

'Appu will not cross this threshold while I am alive.'

He walked home without letting go of Appukkuttan's hand. The people gathered at the bottom of the stairs of the Party Office, dispersed. Ramanan went back to the sewing machine and resumed work.

'Let go of my hand, Father.' Appukkuttan said again. He let go. Appukkuttan was relieved.

As soon as he reached home, he lay down on the bed. He felt that he should not have shouted at Bhargavan the way he had. What crime did Bhargavan commit? He felt as if someone had rescued him at the point of drowning, and, had laid him down. He breathed easy, as if the water clogging his lungs had drained away.

Appukkuttan sat in the verandah, uncomprehending. He sat there as if it was someone else's house. There were red bruises on his hand as if it had been gripped by a pair of pliers. He could not understand why his father had become so agitated.

Father and son didn't speak to each other for the rest of the day. Both of them were immersed in thought. When his father lit the evening lamp in the front verandah, he washed his hands and face and sat reciting his evening prayer.

'Appu, are you angry with your father?'

Appukkuttan's eyes welled up suddenly.

'Is your hand hurt badly?'

Ananthakrishnan picked up his hand, put it in his lap and stroked it softly. Appukkuttan felt as if the roughness of his hand had vanished and the softness had returned.

'Appu, you are a small boy. This is the time for study. My son, please pay attention to your studies.'

'Aren't I the first in the class now?'

'You should stay on top always. You must not fail in any of the tests. You must not become like your father.'

'Which test did you fail, Accha?'

'The test called life.'

He served Appukkuttan rice. And ladled out fish curry from the bowl on top of the rice. Then he poured out warm water in a glass and put that in front of him.

'Shall I roast a pappadam for you, my dear?'

'No, Father.'

'Why don't you eat the rice, then?'

'I am not hungry.'

Managing to eat a little rice and drinking up the water, Appukkuttan rose. Ananthakrishnan ate from the same plate. After washing the plate, the bowl and the glasses and dousing the oven with water, he came back again to his son's side.

'Are you feeling sleepy, my dear?'

'Umm.'

'May Father say something? You must listen to it carefully.'

Appukkuttan looked at his father's face keenly.

'My dear! You must never share your father's fate. That's why I am telling you this now. You should never go to the Party Office from now on. Will you go?'

'No,' said Appukkuttan. 'I'll go only when I grow big.'

He looked at Appukkuttan's face helplessly. Was he praying silently for him not to grow up and remain a child forever?

Appukkuttan didn't understand why his father was forbid him from going to the Party Office. Besides him, there were so many others who sat there every day. On some evenings, he could not even find a place to sit. Not only autorickshaw drivers and beedi rollers, even teachers and officers were daily visitors there. Not merely to discuss politics; people came there to read and to borrow books as well.

On a previous occasion when Appukkkuttan had visited around noon, he found that the Party Office was decorated with red festoons and streamers. Red flags were fluttering on the windows and on top of the roof. There were so many people crowded around there that Appukkuttan couldn't even climb the stairs.

When the Party Secretary Bhargavan came, all of them got down and lined up. Those who were standing on the roadsides and the shop-verandahs also joined them. Suddenly it swelled into a big crowd.

The Secretary and Aaman Sir, who were standing in front, unfurled a red banner and held it up between them. There were red flags in the hands of those who were standing behind them.

The procession moved forward, raising slogans.

Hesitating for a brief moment, Appukkuttan ran up and joined the rear of the procession. Appukkuttan was the youngest participant of the procession.

Long Live the Revolution!
Long Live the Martyrs!
We are the ones who shed blood
We are the ones who caught the bullets
We'll never, never, never be vanquished.

Pumping his fist into the air, Appukkuttan also shouted slogans. A youngster with a stubby beard stood near him. In a coarse voice, he shouted:

We're the children of Kayyur
The police and the gun, are mere grass blades for us
Long Live the Martyrs!

Appukkuttan didn't quite understand the slogans he repeated after others. He intended to ask Aaman Sir about their meaning.

It was his father that Appukkuttan would ask questions to, earlier. Often, the questions he shot perplexed and confused Ananthakrishnan: Why don't males give birth? Why don't chicks fly, although they have wings? Why don't trains run along the roads? Why is Moosath so tall? Why is Visalakshi

Ezhuthamma so dwarfish? What is the difference between a raktasaakshi (martyr) and a kallasaakshi (false witness)?

Later, his son's questions began to annoy Ananthakrishnan.

'Appu don't ask this and that; go, sit down and study.'

When Appukkuttan approached him with questions, he evaded them.

Now Appukkuttan doesn't ask his father anything. He seeks answers for all his querries from Aaman Sir. Appukkuttan is the only pupil in the class who knows the meanings of words like Revolution, Class War, Bourgeois, Petit Bourgeois, Capitalism, Landlordism, Exploitation and the like. It was Aaman Sir who had explained the meanings of all these words. Aaman Sir had converted answering questions into a fine art.

'Appootta, you've asked me so many questions now. Now let me ask you one question. What will you be when you grow up?'

'A martyr.'

Appukkuttan too had made a fine art of answering questions.

Moving along the road behind the railway station, the procession reached the maidan where boys played football in the evenings. A stage had been erected there using bamboo and plaited coconut palm fronds. Songs Kayamkulam People's Art Club, the theatre troupe that had revolutionised the mass psyche and paved the way for the spread of communism in Kerala were heard over the loudspeakers.

Appukkuttan returned home before the meeting was over.

The next day Aaman Sir asked him, 'Your legs must have ached from all that walking yesterday?'

Appukkuttan hadn't been able to sleep at night because of his aching feet.

'You shouted the slogans so animatedly, Appoottan.' Aaman Sir laughed, adding 'We were observing the Kayyur Martyrs' Day. Have you heard of Kayyur?'

'No.'

'It was through agrarian struggles that communism grew in our land. Morazha, Eleri and Kayyur are renowned for peasant struggles. There was no end to the oppression unleashed on small farmers by landlords and the police. Even if they worked hard, sweating blood in the scorching sun, they were still forced to go hungry. The pittance they got as wages was re-routed to the coffers of the landlords through unjust extortions. Kayyur is a place where farmers organised themselves and fought against such exploitation. Kayyur is in the old Kasargode district. If my memory is right, it was in 1938 that a Farmers' Union was formed there for the first time. Comrades T.V. Kunhambu, Koyithattil Chirukandan, Choorikkadan Krishnan Nair and others were responsible for this. As a result of their efforts, the farmers experienced a new awakening and raised their voices to assert their rights. Would the landlords and the police have tolerated that? They tried to suppress the farmers' struggle at Kayyur. But who can suppress farmers this way? Their struggle blazed forth like wildfire in Kayyur. With that, the police began crack down on the leaders. When the police came armed with guns to shoot and kill, some of the leaders went underground in thick forests. Comrade Nayanar was also among them. Our Nayanar was a young man. He didn't even have a moustache then. O my Appootta, there is no end to the sufferings these leaders went through. So many days they hid themselves, often starving. All through the day, they wandered through the forests. And at night they couldn't sleep a wink because of wild animals. One day when our Nayanar was lying on a rock, a snake slithered up his leg and up to his mouth. If it were any one of us, we would have died of fright. However, the comrades who have set apart their lives for justice and equity don't fear anything at all... That's why the police and the army were unable to suppress the farmers' struggle at Kayyur. They arrested all the comrades. 29 March 1943 is a date that we cannot forget in the history of the class struggles of our land. It was on that day that four comrades were hanged to death in Kannur Jail. Thus comrades Potora Kunhambu, Mathattil Appu, Koyithattil Chirukandan and Pallickal Abu became martyrs...

'I too want to become a martyr.'

Twenty-three

The rain fell incessantly. The roof of Aravindan's old house leaked badly. Water rushed down the walls in streams. On the daubed cowdung floor, water formed little puddles.

The entire roof had become dilapidated. Santha felt anxious that the roof might not bear the onslaught of another south-west or north-east monsoon, and that one day the leaky drenched roof would cave in and collapse.

Santha heaved a long sigh.

When the rain ceased briefly and the sun shone, the sound of clothes being thrashed on washing stones rose from the neighbouring houses.

Aravindan stood atop the embankment, chewing meditatively on a coconut-leaf midrib. Maybe he would take a cursory look at those passing below along the lane. Or maybe not. It was Kesavan who told him that he didn't have to look at everything just because he had eyes. And it was Kesavan who had explained to him that eyes were there not only for seeing, but for not seeing as well.

But everyone who passed through the lane would attract Kesavan's attention. They would try to exchange pleasantries with him. The walkers know by heart that there is along the lane that stretches from Moosath's house to the main road. They know how many houses there are on either side and all those who live in them. They also know how many municipal lamps are there in the lane and where the lamp-posts stand. And that Aravindan stands on the embankment. Aravindan has also become one of the landmarks along the lane.

That's why Moosath stood below the steps of the embankment, craned his neck towards Aravindan's house and called out:

'Hey, why are you not seen today on the embankment?'

Moosath felt that some terrible tragedy had occurred if Aravindan were not to be found on the embankment, even on a single day.

'There's some work to do.'

'For you? What work?'

'My mind is in a turmoil.'

'Why should it be? Do you have a job? Do you have a wife and children? Aren't you really fortunate?'

'Are you making fun of me?'

Aravindan looked sternly at Moosath. Moosath felt that there was something wrong with that stare. So he quit the scene immediately without saying anything more.

An autorickshaw came droning along the lane. Autos coming along that lane, which was frequented only by cows and humans, had become the norm, of late. Autos seem to squeeze along the lane. They could be driven along that way only if the drivers were real acrobats. Aravindan stood on the embankment watching the auto advancing along the lane, emitting smoke, groaning and swaying on both sides, almost touching the mud-walls.

Aravindan saw many interesting sights like this one when he stood on the embankment. When he grew tired or bored, he would imagine hitherto unseen sights. He would try to think how beautiful the world of the blind would be. They envision the world not objectively, but subjectively. For those who see things with their minds, and without the control of their eyes, all sights are beautiful. It's only the blind that enjoy the liberty of sight. Aravindan saw Visalakshi Ezhuthamma only as a dwarfish person. But, a blind man could draw her picture in his mind as he pleased—as a slim, tall or fair person. One of the sights Aravindan imagined in his mind was a marriage procession proceeding from one end of the lane and an autorickshaw advancing from the other. With nadaswaram players in front of the marriage procession. And behind them, relatives and friends of the bride and groom. Among them, the brand new bride, her head downcast, clad in a silk sari, wearing lots of ornaments, her hair decked with jasmine flowers, walking on. While the marriage procession fumbles along the alley with difficulty, suddenly an auto appears from the opposite direction, the foliage that grows on the mud-walls is damaged by the advancing authorickshaw turning around the bend. Tender shoots snap and fall. The autorickshaw and the marriage procession now face each other. Neither the auto nor the marriage procession can proceed, circumventing the other. When they stand like that facing each other, engaged in hot exchanges, there comes Moosath's huge Sindhi cow...

Aravindan could not recall now whether this was a real-life incident or a figment of his imagination.

'It is more likely to be fiction,'Aravindan said to himself. 'Because there are no Sindhi cows in Moosath's house. His cows are the local ones, so thin that their ribs can be seen outside.'

The reference to Sindhi cows problematised the realness of that vision. Certain doubts arose in Aravindan. Such a doubt would never have surfaced in Aravindan if it had been a local cow in the place of the Sindhi cow. Logic is not needed to imagine things. But logic is needed to recognise that the scenes seen in one's imagination are not real ones, Aravindan realised.

'Thanks to the Sindhi cow,'said Aravindan, 'for making me realise that I need logic to understand logic.'

Soliloquising was fast becoming a habit with Aravindan. He knew that it was better to talk to oneself than to others. Saint Francis began to talk to birds when humans failed to understand what he was saying. There were at least birds for Saint Francis to communicate with. When Aravindan opened his mouth to say something, even birds flew away.

'I can talk to myself as I like. I won't fly away anywhere,' Aravindan said to himself. 'It's because they didn't know how to talk to themselves that Samuel Beckett and Ionesco wrote so much about the difficulties of communication,' Aravindan continued. To himself.

Chewing on the green coconut leaf midrib, Aravindan stood gazing into the distance. Since the sights near him caused him pain, he only set his sights afar.

'My dear! If you stay gaze on in this locality, you are not going to be saved. Go somehow, somewhere...cross the sea, to Dubai or Abu Dhabi...' Santha said one day.

'Where's the money for that?'

It was news to her that one needed money to go to Dubai. She gaped at her younger brother.

'I know that Santhechi said so because she loves me,' Aravindan said to himself. 'There isn't enough money for train fare in this house even to go to Madras. How then can one go to Dubai?'

Aravindan spat out the sourness of the green midrib into the lane. He chewed midribs like infants suck their fingers.

'To tell you the truth, I don't think nowadays about job or salary. I get out of the house with bus fare from Santhechi and tell her that I am going to the Employment Exchange and go to the cinema and see the noon shows, sitting in the front rows. The white women without a stitch of clothing on their bodies intoxicate me. I have even forgotten my employment registration number...'

Aravindan went to the well, drew an arecanut-swathe full of water and rinsed his mouth. He poured the rest of the water on his feet. He learned from experience that to cool down the mind one has to pour water on the feet and not on the head.

It was then that Sujatha, standing in the courtyard with washed clothes in a bucket caught Aravindan's attention. She picked up the shirt and the mundu from the bucket and hung it on the clothesline to dry. Then she took a yellow petticoat, shook and straightened it and spread it out on the line. Aravindan felt that that shirt, mundu and petticoat were together telling the story of a conjugal life. Aravindan stood looking at Sujatha intently for some time.

'O wife of the world-renowned writer, so far I called you Sujathachechi. When my affection turned more personal and tender, I called you just 'chechi.' But, from now on, I am going to call you 'hey you!'' Aravindan said to himself.

'You'll see no tenderness in my affection from now on. Hey you, there's absolutely no love lost in me, d'you hear? I have no love lost for you, or your husband. Absolutely no love towards anyone.'

'Which husband?'Aravindan continued his monologue: 'What is he capable of? Except writing and publishing lies? Anyone who watches your face when you come out of your bedroom early in the morning can guess what is wrong. He is one who looks in the sky and dreams. You need a man who has his feet firmly planted on this soil.'

Taking the towel from the eaves and scrubbing himself hard behind the ears, he dumbed down to the courtyard once again. He stood looking at Sujatha with his eyes and mind.

'What's it, Aravindan?'

'Nothing.'

'Kesavettan went to the office quite early today. Therefore, my washing and bathing is done early too.'

'Good,' said Aravindan to himself. 'It's God who sent away Kesavan early from the house today. How can the One above fail to see what is going on in my mind? You too must know what is going on in my mind. Oh, no. Why should I describe the Pooram festival that you are anyway going to see for yourself, as the saying goes? Just you watch what I am going to do.'

'What are you staring so intently for, Aravindan?'

'It's nothing. Just like that...'

'No, there's something. Won't you tell your chechi?'

Though Aravindan abruptly withdrew his gaze from Sujatha, his mind was glued to her body like a fly.

Walking beside the chilli bush and the chicken coop, he reached Sujatha's side. After spreading out all the clothes to dry, she picked up the empty bucket in her hand. When Aravindan moved towards that wet yellow petticoat, its cord touched his face.

As he walked behind Sujatha, he continued his interior monologue: 'What I am going to do is something you can't even imagine. When you return after putting away the bucket in the bathroom and enter the kitchen, I will also come in there from the verandah. We will stand like the marriage procession and the autorickshaw in the lane, facing each other. It will become impossible for you to get past me, or me to get past you. But I won't give you time even to stand dazed. Your body, on which the memories of the yellow petticoat sleep, will have been trapped in my hands.'

As Sujatha stepped into the bathroom with the bucket, Aravindan walked up to the verandah.

'When the writer returns in the evening, make a cup of strong tea and give it to him. And then tell him what your neighbour Aravindan, who goes about without a job, did to you. Don't you ever expect him to rush at me with a machete! Your husband, the world-famous writer, is a spineless worm.'

Aravindan got in and waited for Sujatha's return. After two moments, she came and stood facing him, the scent of wet hair hanging between them.

'What an intense stare! What's with you today?'

'I can't bear it, Chechi. I feel like dying.'

'That's better,' said Kesavan. 'No one will lose anything if someone like you, who is not even worth a paise, dies.'

Kesavan who had left early for office, had also returned early.

Twenty-four

Appukkuttan had a defect of vision.

Sitting in the classroom, he could not read anything that was written on the blackboard. Letters appeared to turn into big, red ants. He couldn't see things near him; but he can see things in the distance.

'Great men are like that,' joked Aaman Sir. 'They'll see only things that are far.'

It was Aaman Sir who detected Appukkuttan's problem. He was adept at spotting others' problems.

When he said that he may have to wear glasses, Appukkuttan felt happy. EMS also wore glasses.

'At what age did EMS begin to wear glasses?'

'That...'

Aaman Sir could not answer Appukkuttan's question. He knows by rote the history of the Communist Party and farmers' struggles. He also knows the biographies of the Party leaders. Yet he didn't have the answer to the question as to at what age EMS began to wear glasses. He told himself that all knowledge is incomplete.

'Don't you know, Aaman Sir?'

'No.'

'Eeyyemmes began to wear glasses at the age of twenty-one.'

'How did you know, Appootta?'

Appukkuttan could not answer. Some knowledge is not imparted by anyone; it is born by itself. This knowledge had formed itself in Appukkuttan at that very instant.

Aaman Sir said that at times such revelations happened to him as well.

Aaman Sir went to Ananthakrishnan's house after a long gap.

He didn't go there frequently anymore. The reason is Ananthakrishnan's strange behaviour. When he saw Aaman Sir, Ananthakrishnan developed an expression as if one had been touched by a rat snake. Aaman Sir would want to flee that instant to some place. He sensed that some worry was constantly gnawing at Ananthakrishnan. Once, he was about to ask him about it. Then Aaman Sir withdrew himself from curiosity...

Why ask? He knew everything...

Aaman Sir was least interested in Ananthakrishnan or his life. Let him live howsoever he likes. Let even a cobra, not to speak of a rat snake, wind around his feet...

Aaman Sir's interest was only in Appukkuttan.

But today he must see Ananthakrishnan. This was the question of the light of Appukkuttan's eyes. That light shouldn't go dim.

When Aaman Sir arrived, Ananthakrishnan was sitting there mending the mundu, sewing its torn end. He shuddered visibly seeing Aaman Sir. Withdrawing both his feet, he hid them under the bench he sat on. One would imagine that Aaman Sir had come to take away Ananthakrishnan's legs.

Although Ananthakrishnan didn't invite him to take a seat, Aaman Sir sat down on the bench beside him. At that instant, the bench shook like Ananthakrishnan's legs. Aaman Sir gives everyone the shudders.

'It's quite some time since I came here. What to do? Where's the time?'

Pausing his sewing, Ananthakrishnan pricked up his ears.

'Appoottan must be taken to an eye specialist. His eyes should be tested. I suspect he has a problem with his vision.'

'There is nothing wrong with Appu's eyesight.'

'Of course, there is. He can't see anything that's written on the blackboard.'

Thinking it over for a moment, he said, 'I'll take him to Koman Vaidyar. That's enough.'

Sometime ago Appukkuttan had had an attack of conjunctivitis. Both his eyes turned red, as if to turn Marxist overnight. When he woke up in the morning, both his eyes were sealed shut with scum, rendering it impossible for him to open them. It was Koman Vaidyar who had treated Appukkuttan then. When the Vaidyar's medicine hit the eyes, the world would blaze away. For some time, day would turn into night.

'It's not enough just to take him to the Vaidyar, Anantheshna. He may have to wear glasses.'

'To get glasses, we have to go to town.'

'Don't take the trouble yourself, Anantheshna. I'll take Appoottan.'

'No.'

'What is it Anantheshna? Am I an outsider?'

'Sir, you have taken a lot of trouble for my son. You shouldn't do that any more. I'll look after Appu's affairs myself from now on.'

'It's no trouble at all for me. It's a matter of great pleasure for me to be able to do anything for Appukkuttan. He is now first in the class. If he continues like this, he will secure First Rank in the SSLC exams. These things give me pleasure.'

Ananthakrishnan sat looking at the floor, wordlessly. Slowly, he took out the legs he had hidden under the bench and stretched them. Now his gaze rested on his own feet.

Finally Ananthakrishnan agreed. He disliked yet liked Aaman Sir at the same time.

Sitting in the bus, Aaman Sir told Appukkuttan:

'You should always read sitting in the light. And eat a lot of vegetables.'

Appukkuttan rejoiced inwardly because of his diminished eyesight. He had wished to wear glasses like EMS. That wish was now being fulfilled. What if the eye doctor said that there was no need for glasses? That was the only fear he had now.

'It's in our country that the greatest number of people with defective vision are found. The reason is the deficiency of vitamins in our diet. Only in a socialist setup will there be perfect eyesight for all.'

Aaman Sir continued after a while, as the sat in the town bus, rumbling slowly forward.

'The elections are round the corner. Everyone says that I must contest. The Party will allot me only a sure-fire winning seat. But my conscience doesn't permit me to give up this job of teaching children.'

'Can't you contest the elections without giving up the job?'

'That's not possible, Appootta. Either school master or an MLA; one can't be both at the same time, according to the rules.'

Appukkuttan felt angry at 'the rules'.

'Let the Party decide. I'll obey the Party. That's it.'

'Is Eeyyemmes an MLA?'

'Why should Eeyyemmes need an MLA's postion? His place is in the hearts of the hundreds of thousands of people.'

Getting off in the town, they drank lemonade to quench their thirst and walked along the road. There is an eye-specialist known to Aaman Sir opposite Chitravani cinema.

Both Appukkuttan and Aaman Sir felt very happy walking together down the road together.

It was the first time after the day when Ananthakrishnan had dragged Appukkuttan home from the Party Office that they had come together to town.

Appukkuttan had once gone to Chitravani along with his father for a matinee. He remembered that after the show, they had gone to Hotel Jayabharati for dal vadas and hot tea. The heroine of the film Appukkuttan had seen that day was also called Jayabharati. Appukkuttan liked films with sad themes. He liked to share the sorrow of the hero and the heroine and wept along with them.

City Opticals was located above a motor spare-parts' shop. There was a Sikh standing in the shop, wearing a turban like the towel Ananthakrishnan wrapped around his head when he went out on misty January mornings. Why do the Sikhs cover their heads? Was there dewfall in their land all the time and not just in January? Taking out an iron-toothed wheel with an attached spring from his bag, he began to speak to the shop-owner in a mixture of English, Hindi and Malayalam. Appukkuttan was eager to have a look at the other spare part in his bulging bag. But Aaman Sir ascended the stairs, without stopping there, holding his hand. There was mildew on the cement railing.

All the employees of City Opticals smiled genially when they saw Aaman Sir.

'This is Appoottan. My student. His eyes have to be tested.'

'What TV do you have at home? Local or imported?'

The ophthalmologist was a wiry, diminutive man. There was no comparison between his body and that of Koman Vaidyar who poured burning medicine into one's eyes. He reminded one not of Moosath, but of Visalakshi Ezhuthamma.

'Don't you watch TV?'

'No.'

'Why?'

'My father doesn't have enough money to buy a TV.'

'Why do you need money? Everything is now available on instalments.'

'My father doesn't like TV.'

'And you?'

'I like TV.'

'That's why your eyes got damaged. You must be sitting in the neighbour's houses and watching TV, right?'

The eye specialist laughed. He flashed a torch into Appukuttan's eyes like a torchlight into a dark alley at night. It was the first time Appukkuttan had seen such a small torch. Ordinarily, when the light of a torch is flashed into one's eyes, one would naturally blink. But when the beam of light from the doctor's torch shone into his eye, Appukkuttan did not blink at all. He didn't even know that there was light falling onto his eyes. He decided that he would buy a torch like that some time in the future.

The eye specialist made Appukkuttan read the letters on a board hung on the wall. He didn't find it difficult to read the big letters on top. When he reached the smaller letters below, he fumbled like when he read the letters on the blackboard in the classroom.

'You should have come a little earlier. Never mind. It'll be all right, he is still a boy.'

After the eye test, he rang a bell and ordered tea. The three of them drank strong, hot tea, bitter due to the small amount of milk. After that, he opened the draw, took out a cigarette and put it between his lips. And gave Aaman Sir one too.

'When did you start this?' asked Aaman Sir.

The doctor laughed, blowing smoke from his nostrils and mouth.

'I know that it's bad. TV spoils the eyes. And cigarettes, the chest. But do we do certain things weighing the good and evil involved? I ask the children coming here with bad eyes, whether they watch TV. Just that. I never tell anyone not to watch TV. Let them decide that. My job is fixing the eyes of the patients coming to me. Just that. Advising all and sundry, preaching morality and so on is not my business.'

He didn't accept the fees Aaman Sir offered him.

'The doctor is an interesting fellow. He is a good man. But we can't agree with much of what he says.'

There was something about the eye specialist Appukkuttan liked very much.

After two days, Aaman Sir himself went to the town and bought a pair of spectacles for Appukkuttan.

Putting them on, Appukkuttan went over to the mirror and looked at himself. Hair combed to one side, thick-framed glasses and a hard, dark face...

The young EMS.

Twenty-five

Aaman Sir doesn't know how to dream. He tends to live among realities.

'I don't understand it when you talk about 'dreams about the future." He said sitting in the Party Office. 'The future is to be built, not to be dreamt about.'

That was the title of an article he wrote recently in *Desabhimani*—'Building the Future.' He had tried to establish in the article, that the future was something to be built, much like a hydro-electric project or a steel plant. He had explained dreams as offshoots of weaknesses or disease.

He told the comrades in the Party Office: 'It's not dreams, but scientifically prepared blueprints and hard work that are needed for big projects. If those who build dams base their work on dreams, they will come crashing down in a couple of days.'

On another occasion Aaman Sir told Appukkuttan: 'It's because our people are dreamy and lazy that socialism and communism have been delayed in being established in our country. We have a future only if we can destroy the dreams of the middle classes and bring them down to the realm of work.'

Earlier, when Aaman Sir spoke, Appukkuttan wouldn't understand a thing. But nowadays, he had begun to understand little bits of what he said. And yet, Appukkuttan couldn't grasp what he said so seriously about dreams.

'Do you dream, Appootta?'

'In my sleep.'

'The dreams that we see in our sleep will do no harm. What I said was not about them. I was talking about the daydreams we see have when we are awake. These daydreams are dangerous.'

'I don't have daydreams at all.'

'Very good!' Aaman Sir congratulated Appukkuttan, patting his shoulder.

What does Aaman Sir think about when he is walking alone? Doesn't his solitude lead him by the hand to dreams?

But then, it is rare that Aaman Sir is alone. When he goes to school, on the bus or in the Party Office, he is always talking to someone. He is interested more in making others talk and listening to them. That's the style he employs even in the classroom. He makes bright students take classes for the rest of the class. That's how Appukkuttan began to teach his own classmates.

Once when Aaman Sir was standing in front of the Party Office, Kamala had passed by. When she passed the tailor Ramanan's shop, she didn't even pretend to have seen him; neither did she talk to him.

Aaman Sir, who knew about their relationship, said, 'Kamala, stop.'

Kamala stopped.

'Ramanan, talk to Kamala.'

Aaman Sir told Ramanan that it was not right that they did not speak to each other, even when they met. It should not happen that way, he said. Aaman Sir surprised Ramanan. The relationship between Ramanan and Kamala was one that the people didn't approved of. They belonged to different castes. It was because they were afraid of the opposition that they pretended not to notice each other in public.

'Do not meet and talk clandestinely. Both of you are adults. Ramanan, you have enough means to support a woman. Why can't you both go to the Registrar's Office and marry? I'm with you.'

That's the way Aaman Sir speaks to people.

Ramanan asked Aaman Sir why he had not married yet, even though he had begun to grey around the temples.

'Why, will I not be able to feed a woman? Am I lacking in health? And yet I haven't married, only because I have decided not to. There are some other important things to be done with my life. I don't get enough time even for that. I don't feel that marriage is a necessity. I know what's in your mind when I tell you so. You want to know how I'll satisfy my bodily needs, don't you? My dear man, I don't feel that kind of an urge. The body will demand only what is in our mind. In my mind there are other urges. A wife and a family are not among them mind you.'

Aaman Sir thinks about himself only very rarely. All his thoughts revolve around the land and its people.

However, the people cram their heads with more thoughts about him than are necessary. They do not understand the secret behind Aaman Sir's bachelorhood. They have a burning curiosity to understand more about that. The explanations that Aaman Sir gives now and then don't convince them. Some see incongruity in such a senior person going about with Appukkuttan. Why does he make friends with such a small boy? People looked on amazed as they walk, talking and laughing, he with his hand on the shoulder of Appukkuttan, who doesn't even reach his shoulder. Can't he keep the company of other teachers, who are his age? Can't he keep the company of Appukkuttan's father, if he wants?

Aaman Sir, who hails from another locality, came there for the first time when he got a job in the school. He had got the job in Appukkuttan's school without paying any bribe. People know that it was the influence of his Party that was behind it. There is nothing that he doesn't know about this locality and the people. Even Ananthakrishnan, who was born and brought up here, doesn't know so much about this area. Ananthakrishnan doesn't know who is related to whom and who lives where. Aaman Sir has a special ability to recognise people at first sight and to remember their family relations.

'We will understand ourselves only if we know the society we live in,' Aaman Sir said, once.

'There isn't any place where that Aaman Sir's eyes don't reach,' said Moosath. 'There isn't anything that he doesn't see.'

In fact Aaman Sir uses his eyes more to look than to see. He described to Appukkuttan the difference between seeing and looking: 'Appootta, our eyes can see everything, irrespective of what we like to see. But looking is not like that. We'll see only what we want to see when we look. There is an effort involved in looking. And there should be an interest as well.

One's culture, politics and other things can be read from the way one looks.'

It was by looking that he found that Padmavathy had distanced herself from Appukkuttan.

'Appootta, is Padmavathy angry with you?'

'She is angry with everyone.'

Appukkuttan fixed his glasses that were slipping down his nose. Onlookers got the feeling that he was not a boy but a grown up, when he looked over the lenses of his glasses.

'D'you know? Padmavathy liked you...'

'She doesn't like anyone.'

'But she liked you.'

'Haven't you got anything else to tell me, Sir?'

Appukkuttan didn't at all wish to talk about such light-hearted matters.

Aaman Sir believes that it is good for Appukkuttan to have a little girl companion at his age. He knows that the people or parents wouldn't approve of it. The world takes very harsh stands in the case of man-woman relationships. Though Ramanan and Kamala had reached adulthood so long ago and had the maturity to decide what to do with their lives and to carry out their decisions, they saw each other only surreptitiously. They exchange a few words only after hiding themselves from others' prying eyes?

'Not only struggles and conflict, even armed revolt for getting rights established had been recognised by the society nowadays,' said Aaman Sir. 'But in the matter of man-woman relationships, society will not recognise any rights. We are very rigid about this matter.'

'We are Malayalees,' said Bhargavan.

'Bhargavan, in a socialist setup, there isn't a class called Malayalees. There are only two classes: the haves and the have-nots.'

Could the society that didn't approve of the relationship of the mature Ramanan and Kamala, brook the relationship of Appukkuttan and Padmavathy, who were children?

'Appootta, I have told you many things. Whenever I learn something, I have exchanged it with you. What is the use? You are basically an ordinary boy. An ordinary boy whose face flushes upon hearing the name of a girl....'

Aaman Sir bent down and looked at Appukkuttan's face. A tall person like him had to bend over to see the face of a boy like Appukkuttan.

'Have you touched Padmavathy?'

'Yes.'

'When?'

'Earlier we used to go to school holding hands.'

Aaman Sir laughed till his sides ached. The movement of that laughter travelled from his right shoulder to his left shoulder and back to right shoulder.

'Appootta, you can decide what to do and what not to do when you grow up. That's what I do now. It's my mind that controls the movements of my body. And it is my political sense that controls my mind.'

Let Appukkuttan live like a boy until he grows up. Let him study, play and eye the girls in the class.

'Go and play some games in the evening. Your classmates are playing football. Why don't you play with them, Appootta?'

'I want only to walk with you, Sir.'

'There is an age gap of about thirty years between us.'

Precious moments pass as Appukkuttan walks with Aaman Sir in the evenings along the paddy fields and river banks. It has become something of a habit with him. Appukkuttan could not sleep if that walk was not taken, even for a day.

Aaman Sir walked along, holding Appukkuttan's hand. He drew himself up to his full height, he would grow up as big as Aaman Sir. While Aaman Sir bent over to be closer to Appukkuttan's size.

Aaman Sir was sure that Appukkuttan would be a youth with a powerful intellect and a firm mind. He would be a communist who loves humanity. Aaman Sir was a small-time communist, who wished to die after moulding a big Communist. Will Appukkuttan fulfil that wish?

'Let's go to the Party Office, Sir.'

'We *are* going there.'

Twenty-seven

Dear teachers, students,

You know that I am one who has always avoided speeches in public. I did so not only because words lose their privacy on platforms, but also because I have nothing to tell anyone. I fear that when I say this you will be perplexed and, perhaps, look upon me as a hypocrite. We are living in the midst of a deluge of news and information created by new technology. And yet, I do not have anything to tell you? No. I recognise with a shudder the political, ecological and cultural calamities taking shape all around me. And yet, do I wish to stand mute before you? Yes. But I pray to you with all my heart not to read this muteness of mine as a sign of my inability to react, or as an apolitical stand.

I am a novelist and short storywriter. It is also true that I used to scribble some poetry many years ago. But it has been two decades since I last wrote a poem. Therefore, I dare not call myself a poet. It is totally irrelevant as to what name others have given me or what they want me to be seen as. You must seek relevance not in me, but only in my writings. It is not your problem what I, Kesavan, do, think or dream about. Let me suffer terribly from syphilis like Gaugin; let me suffer hellish agony in lunacy like Artaud. These do not affect you in any way. There is one reason why I state this here repeatedly. I received an anonymous letter a couple of days ago. That reader, who did not dare to declare his own name and to put down his signature, has discovered the root cause of all my problems, both material and spiritual. This is what he wrote to me. 'Kesavan, the root cause of all your problems is that you are unable to satisfy your wife in bed.'

Ever since I began the writing of my new novel, I have been receiving such anonymous letters. I do not ignore as trifles these letters that do not carry the name or address of their senders. They are not to be discarded. These letters communicate to me at a deeper level. For instance, look at this letter I received last week. Hear what is written: 'Hey, you, Kesavan! Why do you write a novel about EMS? Could you think of only *this* Sankaran—Elamkulam Manackal Sankaran—to write a novel about, in this land where Adi Sankaran was born?' Why don't I consign these anonymous letters to the wastepaper basket? Mainly for one reason. Because, in anonymous letters, I see the purity of ideas and transparency of language. I believe that anonymous letters take shape not in the head, but in the heart. Each anonymous letter is an explosion of originality. It is a scream from the periphery of intellect and reason. A philosopher presents an idea that germinates in his mind, however tiny it may be, in the form of an essay, connecting it with many other ideas and exploring the possibilities of language. There is a line I underscored in Levinas's *Otherwise Than Being or Beyond Essence*: 'Satisfaction satisfies itself with satisfaction.' The writer of an anonymous letter attains satisfaction not this way; it is through a scream. Unlike many others do, I do not find any cowardice involved in the writing of anonymous letters. I do not see any obscenity or ribaldry in it. If we exhibit language together with its usual appendages and ornaments, they appear obscene or ribald. And yet that is not really so. Even if I am able to recognise the authors of the anonymous letters I receive, I don't send them a reply. Because, anonymous letter-writers are interested only in throwing their thoughts and emotions at us. It is none of their concern, or obligation, to find out what we throw back at them. They wish only to scream aloud. They do not expect from us a scream in return.

My inadequacies regarding protesting and taking positions have been pointed out time and again by lovers of literature—critics like my friend Ravunni and some thinkers. I would like to remind you that this is a wrong, unjustifiable, allegation. Because each sentence you see in the novels and stories I write are manifestations of the positions I take. You must not look for beauty or aesthetic experience in a literary work. And these positions need not be political, philosophical or ideological. Because life is not philosophy and ideology alone. My friends level an accusation at me: that I do not even participate in demonstrations against religious fundamentalism and ecological devastation. Please do not entertain the misunderstanding that it is because I am personally in favour of such concepts that I do not participate in such demonstrations. It is because I am unable to exhibit the articles of my faith on public platforms, processions and protest marches and in front of TV cameras. I do not wish to become the propagandist of my own beliefs, however small or big they may be. I must recognise the truth that the externalisation of ideas would lead me to an elephantine trap. We must realise that externalisation will gradually nullify those very ideas. Popular TV channels and newspapers and magazines that have a large circulation carry our ideas directly to those who are unable to share them or who are proponents of ideas that run counter to ours, and thus create conflicts. These conflicts created by the media will only help in disturbing the credo we hold close to our hearts. Counter-ideas are never harmful. It is our unending hunger for externalisation that weakens our original thoughts and adds muck to our language. Let me remind you that it is *not* to convince you that I boycott public platforms, that I have spoken so much on this subject.

As to whether I must write the novel about Adi Sankaran or Elamkulam Manakkal Sankaran Namboodiripad, is a question of choice. When I do not write about Adi Sankaran and write about Sankaran Namboodiripad, my position becomes clear. This position doesn't require a Preface or Appendix. To explain this position of mine, I do not require a public platform, newspapers, magazines or TV cameras.

If I am not a good performer in bed, it is a matter that concerns only my wife, or, if I have concubines, them. This should, by no means, affect writers, philosophers or ideologues.

I am a clerk. Let me live on, pushing files in the office, and writing a story or a novel from time to time. If I die, no one must institute an award in my name. No one must unveil my portrait in the Akademi Hall. I would like to remain without a name or address, like an anonymous letter-writer. Because, writing, to me, is the scream of an anonymous letter-writer.

Many thanks to you for patiently listening to these rantings of one who has nothing to say. I conclude my speech, with love for all.

Twenty-eight

SSLC examinations were round the corner, killing the sleep of parents, spraying embers in the minds of students and sowing seeds of general unease in homes. Even past midnight, the light would remain switched on in one room. Sometimes, that light went out for some time and shone again well before the first cock crowed.

Ananthakrishnan was in a dilemma, now. His mind grew turbulent. He had told Aaman Sir that he didn't have any great dreams about Appukkuttan. That's what he used to tell everyone, all the time. Ananthakrishnan only wished to see Appukkuttan become a clerk when he grew up. But he didn't remember that for someone to even become a clerk these days was in itself a big dream. Even if he needs only a clerk's job, doesn't he have to pass the examinations, scoring high marks? Doesn't he have to write tests and top the ranks?

Can Appukkuttan pass the SSLC without Aaman Sir's help?

Questions such as these confused Ananthakrishnan.

His conscience didn't permit him to go to Aaman Sir once again, begging him to save Appukkuttan. He curled up and lay like a tortoise feigning death, withdrawing into its shell. In a bout of self-pity, he saw only tragedies approaching in his life.

And, at that moment, Aaman Sir walked up to him.

There was an overwhelming sense of self-confidence in his gaze and gait. No one has ever seen him falter or hesitate.

It was after a very long time that Aaman Sir was coming to his house. Ananthakrishnan felt as if God Himself had sent him there, harking to his cry. His body shuddered a little.

Without leaving his sandals at the entrance-steps as usual, Aaman Sir marched up to the verandah as if entering his own house.

'If you do not like my coming here, you must tell me so openly now.'

'Ayyo—who said I don't like your coming here?'

'One can understand certain things without being told as much.' Aaman Sir laughed. The derision hidden behind that laughter did not go unnoticed by Ananthakrishnan.

Ananthakrishnan tried so hard to separate Appukkuttan from Aaman Sir. He had even fallen at Aaman Sir's feet. And yet, now, when the examinations were at hand, he was seeking his help. Ananthakrishnan fumbled for words.

Everything was for Appu—for his future.

'Sir...'

'Don't say anything now. I know everything. I'll help Appoottan.'

'I'll be obliged to you for ever. If I have spoken uncivil words to you, it was for Appu's sake. We are both trying to do the same thing. And our aim is the same—Appu's welfare.'

'But Appoottan is not my son.'

Aaman Sir felt a deep loathing towards Ananthakrishnan. He was so selfish. He had no qualms about changing the colours of opinions and ideas to suit the dictates of the occasion. When he said 'Appu's welfare,' he only meant his own.

'You are disgusted with me, aren't you? Sir, I am a poor man. Living on with a little devotion to God and cooking for our little family.' He continued after a brief pause: 'Please help my son to secure a top rank. I shall fall at your feet a hundred times…'

He bent over to touch Aaman Sir's feet. Aaman Sir drew his feet back.

Aaman Sir was confused. Was Ananthakrishnan such a simpleton with a flexible spine? How could such a person have become an armed revolutionary? Ananthakrishnan eluded his comprehension.

Carefully concealing his abhorrence for Ananthakrishnan, Aaman Sir said:

'Padmavathy is weak in English. I am going to give her tuition. Let Appoottan come to her house. I'll teach both of them together.'

Ananthakrishnan could not believe his own ears. He felt like he should pay obeisance to Aaman Sir once again.

'Appootta, for now, no more library and reading room for you. Reading weeklies and novels is no longer allowed. Tuition will begin, from tomorrow. Come to Padmavathy's house at five sharp.'

Aaman Sir got up and without bidding farewell or looking at Ananthakrishnan's face, walked away.

Padmavathy was disturbed when she learned that Appukkuttan was coming to her house for tuition. The spout of the bronze *kindi* kept at the edge of the verandah got caught in the hem of her skirt and she tumbled into the courtyard. The coir rope slipped from her hand when she was drawing water from the well, and raced down the pulley with the bucket attached to its other end and crashed into the well; when she ironed her father's shirt, the collar got burned; and when she warmed milk, it boiled over into the oven. All these calamities occurred within the space of a half hour.

Padmavathy's father was not like Ananthakrishnan. When she maintained that she didn't want tuition, in a rather adamant fashion, he wordlessly pulled out the cane he had kept inserted in the thatches. He didn't hesitate to wallop his daughter with a cane, even though she was sixteen. Padmavathy, who had no fear of Parassinikkadavu Muttappan, was paralysed with fear about her father's cane. All her courage would drain away. If not for that cane, tucked away in the eaves, she would never have consented to sit together with Appukkuttan for tuition.

Appukkuttan didn't have any such issues. Hatred or vengeance do not raise their heads in his mind. If they do, he doesn't know how to maintain them. He never even once felt that Padmavathy was a problem that beset him.

There were certain other thoughts in Appukkuttan's mind. Once the examinations were over, he must go to Valluvanad on a pilgrimage and visit Elamkulam Mana. Before setting foot inside the compound of Elamkulam Mana, he must touch the earth there, and then, with the dust on his fingers, touch the crown of his head. After his mother's death, EMS had shifted to Pulinkavu, after donating all his property to the Party. Appukkuttan knew this had happened in 1936. Elamkulam Mana and Pulinkavu are pilgrimage centres for him.

Appukkuttan had only recently visited Pokkan's house in Mavilaayi, where EMS had gone underground in 1940. Thrills rippled all over Appukkuttan's body as he set foot in the hut where EMS had lived, reading and writing.

It was Aaman Sir who told Appukkuttan stories of peasant struggles, police atrocities, of the leaders' lives filled with sacrifices and of martyrs. But now, it was through books that he perfected his knowledge and acquired new knowledge. He spent all the money that he had to buy books from Chintha Publications. The histories of struggles and the biographies of leaders nestle next to his text books.

Reading these books, unnoticed by his father, he fell sleep at night.

Appukkuttan, who didn't remember even his own date of birth, could reel off accurately the dates of struggles and strikes. Appukkuttan knew that it was in 1939 that N.G. Ranga, the President of All India Kissan Sabha, came to Malabar and rejuvenated the farmers' movement. It happened before either Aaman Sir or Appukkuttan were born.

Farmland to the farmers
Down with zamindari

Appukkuttan knew this slogan was first raised in Malabar on 16 September, 1938.

As he slept with the books of Prabhat Book House and Chintha Publications resting on his chest, Appukkuttan travelled through the milieux of the struggles of agricultural labourers. Appukkuttan felt that he was also standing among the farmers' leaders who gathered for discussions in the house of Naniyoor

Vishnu in Kolachery on 12 July, 1935. Appukkuttan also clapped his hands as Comrade Keraleeyan was elected the Secretary of the Farmers' Union. When, under the leadership of T.V. Kunhambu, the Farmers' March that marked the beginning of the Kayyur Struggle moved towards Kookot, Appukkuttan also joined in, raising slogans and crossing paddy fields. When the convicts in the Kayyur Case, Koyithattil Chirukandan, Potora Kunhambu and Mathattil Appu, were hanged on 8 March, 1943 at Kannur Central Jail, Appukkuttan shed tears standing among the comrades who thronged outside the jail. Comrades P.C. Joshi and Sundaraiya, standing on either side of him, consoled Appukkuttan. Tears rolled down P.C. Joshi's left eye.

Appukkuttan's days were set apart for school, and nights, for journeys through the bloody battles of his land.

Appukkuttan inscribed the prefix 'Comrade' to his name on his text books and copy books. His classmates and teachers were not at all amazed to see this. Because they had been referring to him as 'Comrade Appukkuttan' from much earlier on, unbeknownst to him. They did so to make fun of him. Some called him 'Comrade Appukkuttan' to his face, to provoke him. But instead of being provoked, he was filled with joy by such an address.

After becoming a 'Comrade', Appukkuttan had a desire.

'Are you a member of the Party, Sir?'

'Of course!'

'At what age can one become a Party member?'

'When you attain adulthood.'

'Can I too become a Party member when I become an adult?'

'Not a mere member; you'll become a leader of the Party. You may even become a Central Committee Member or even the General Secretary of the Party.'

Appukkuttan would be beside himself with joy hearing this.

He didn't want to become a doctor or engineer. Neither did he want to become a clerk, in accordance with his father Ananthakrishnan's wish. He wanted to become a leader. A leader who leads marches and addresses hundreds of thousands of people.

Like EMS.

Twenty-nine

Saravanan had been drinking non-stop, as he had a windfall that day after some Gulf-employed person had tossed a hundred rupee note at him. He had not set his eyes on such a big amount of money in quite a while. By noon, his bowels, which had shrunk away without proper food for so long, were filled with arrack. When the glass touched his lips, arrack dripped from his mouth like when a pot full of water is filled again. His hands, ribs and the straggling beard were soaked in arrack.

Saravanan, sitting every day on the parapet of the culvert for such a long time, has become a part of it. The culvert, the kanjiram tree near it and the wall behind the tree, on which graffittied slogans and posters abound, form Saravanan's permanent abode.

Even though several years have passed, the sharpness of Saravanan's tongue hasn't diminished any. His tongue today is a dagger he keeps in his mouth. There is no change in Saravanan's talk or behaviour. But his body has shrunk and become somewhat like a coconut-leaf-midrib. His thin, elongated neck appeared to be able to pass through a bangle. There are grey streaks in his hair and beard. He had dispensed with the habit of wearing a shirt altogether. Through the skin, from beneath which flesh and blood had drained away, all his ribs could be seen. He looked as though he had just emerged from a coffin, unseen by anyone.

Saravanan, who was immersed in some thought, didn't see Appukkuttan approaching from far. Appukkuttan had begun to wear a mundu.

With great difficulty, Saravanan got down from the culvert and stood facing the road. He had even more difficulty in keeping his legs straight, swaying as they were in opposite directions. As it was midday, the road was empty. He cleared his throat, as if in preparation to speak into a mike.

Imagining that there was a huge crowd in front of him listening to his every word, Saravanan tightened his hold on the invisible mike, cleared his throat once again and began his speech.

Respected Brothers and Sisters,

I have certain things to tell you. I do not know how to speak it all out and conclude it appropriately. For me, who used to go about delivering speeches in colleges, public places and maidans, it is not possible now to speak even ten sentences effectively.

I have forgotten language. Whatever little of language I have retained, is obscenity. All these years, sitting on this culvert, it was through obscenities that I communicated with you. Now, that is the only language I know.

Let me request you at the very outset not to take my words for a drunkard's ranting and so refrain from lending your ears to what I have to say. Although three-fourths of a bottle of arrack has gone into my stomach, I am facing you in full consciousness. Before my day is done and my tongue silenced, let me tell you what I have to say. I once again request you not to leave thinking that my speech is going to be a long string of abuses; I beg you to listen to my words with rapt attention.

Let me remind you that I was born in a good family and used to go about wearing a clean mundu and shirt daily and had attained MA in Malayalam. If I wanted, I could easily have secured the job of a lecturer, got married, raised children, built a house and lived happily, taking my family to town on holidays, eating in fashionable restaurants. However, the path I chose was different.

I am standing before you at this moment, not to speak about myself. I ceased to be a long time ago. What am I to say about what is not? The reason why I said, by way of a preface, that I was born in a good family and that I am well-educated was only to convince that my words are not merely the babblings from the mouth of a drunkard.

My countrymen, let me now enter the topic of my speech.

Dear Sisters and Brothers, what I've got to tell you is regarding the present political conditions of our land. We have created many martyrs and suffered many sacrifices in the name of politics. The generation that passed before mine had participated in the freedom movement and dedicated their lives for the liberation of the country. Charkha and khadi were the symbols of their dedication. Khadi that was spun on the charkha was the symbol of simplicity and purity. They were the ones who filled the jails, leaving behind the joys of family life, the comforts of their homes, the security of jobs and their very own localities. There were many who sacrificed their lives. The stains of blood and tears that were smeared then on our great country, from Kashmir to Kanyakumari, remain fresh even now.

Finally we got freedom.

Sisters and Brothers, but what was this freedom for?

Freedom to drive a Mercedes Benz, with the hands that turned the charkha?

Freedom to stuff the pockets of the khadi dress with crores earned through corruption?

Freedom to burn alive starving Dalits?

Freedom to maintain power, murdering and pillaging and stoking the fires of caste and religion?

Yes; this is the freedom our past generations won for us.

As if hearing the applause that rose, like the roar of a torrential downpour, Saravanan raised his right hand and appealed to the audience to be silent.

My dear countrymen, the story of freedom doesn't end here.

By the time of my generation, the hammer and sickle and the red flag had occupied the place of charkha and khadi. With the expectations of the second Independence of our country, the sun rose regularly.

That was the real freedom.

Freedom from exploitation and hunger.

Freedom that made social justice and equality possible.

Sisters and Brothers, I will shout for your benefit some slogans that rose in those times:

Farmland to farmers!
Down with zamindari!!
Long Live Unity of the Proletariat!
Long Live the Revolution!!

My dear countrymen! Now listen to the song they sang then:

O the unemployed!
O the sorrow-filled!
O those who spin around!
Like a boat without a rudder...

Dear Sisters and Brothers. Let me now sing for you another song they sang:

O those who thresh the corn
And sow the field
Why this hungry belly...

It was not in the Himalayan foothills or Gangetic plains that this blood-sun of the second Independence rose; it was here, in this Malayalam land of ours.

But what was this freedom for?

Earlier, there were farmlands and farmers here. Now neither are to be seen.

Earlier, there were workers and factories. Now, neither exist here.

The Communists who brought about the second Independence saw one way of eradicating the hunger of the farmer: by eradicating the farmer himself.

The means they found to save labourers, from the exploitation of the employers was to convert the labourers into capitalists.

To end exploitation, they adopted the tactics of converting the exploited into exploiters.

Sisters and Brothers, lend your ears to my words. Pay attention to what I say. I tell you this with the words of my heart:

The Congressmen who brought about the first Independence and the Communists who brought about the second Independence are two sides of the same coin. What they wanted was only power.

You must learn this: Joseph Stalin killed more human beings than Adolf Hitler did. They too are two sides of the same coin.

Comrades, in unison with the soul of Trotsky that hasn't found rest, I curse you.

I curse you—for, your thirst for blood is not yet quenched even after killing off countless humans beings, and so, now you burn alive dumb animals and birds.

A feeble clapping of hands rose from the audience—the audience consisting solely of The Two Drunks squatting in front of him. They lapped up Saravanan's speech and gave him a standing ovation.

My dear two drunks—

Saravanan continued in a weak voice, standing on his drowsy legs:

We three drunks are the creations of the two Independences earned by spilling blood and sacrificing lives. We are one from now on.

Come, drunks.

Let us celebrate our two Independences.

When Saravanan walked towards the wall behind, lifting his mundu, the Two Drunks followed him obediently.

As usual, the wall was full of cinema bills and posters of political parties. Enticing posters of noon shows were also plastered all over. So many posters, showing in so many moods, expressions, colours and poses, film stars like Mammootty, Mohanlal, Murali, Sreenivasan, Mamukoya, Shobhana, Urvasi, Parvathi and others…squeezed in among them, EMS smiled like a baby. The two teeth on the front upper jaw were whiter than the other teeth.

'First I,' said Saravanan: 'Then you, the two drunks.'

Saravanan stood in front of the leader of hundreds of thousands of people, positioned in between film stars. But before he could begin the celebration, two small hands stretched towards him through the flames of the noon sun, grabbed him by the scruff of his neck and shook him all over. Appukkuttan silenced him forever, rendering him unable to slash at anyone anymore with the sharp dagger in his mouth, and he collapsed like a tree with rotten roots, urine streaming down his legs…

Thirty

Ramanan, the tailor can see, sitting in front of his sewing machine, those who are going into the Party Office and those coming out. The people who came up from the Junction had to pass in front of his tailoring shop to go to the Party Office. Ramanan, sitting below and pedalling away on his machine, can hear the discussions and commotion in the Party Office on the second storey. When the Congressmen once threw stones at the Party Office, the first stone, missing the mark, fell on Ramanan's machine. That was the day Ramanan realised that Congressmen were not even close to experts at stone-pelting. How else could a stone, thrown at the Party Office on the second storey, reach his shop, situated at ground-level, to the right?

Ramanan is now a Party sympathiser. He looks at the Red Flag that flutters atop the Party Office with deep love and respect. That flag would appear before him in its many expressions. Sometimes it would fly high and taut, as if to vanquish heaven and earth. During the rainy season, it was seen hanging wet and limp. On the day of the first rains, drops of blood from the new flag fell on the heads and chests of those who passed below the Party Office without umbrellas.

'It is Aaman Sir and the Party who have brought us this happiness. We must never forget Sir or the Party even on pain of death,' Ramanan told Kamala during their 'first night.'

He had vowed an offering of one hundred and one red flags for the Party's District Convention, in return for the favour of uniting him and Kamala in matrimony. After their marriage, he had fulfilled that vow. They had to sell off Kamala's goat to raise money for it. But neither Kamala nor Ramanan were sorry.

'Why should you need the goat anymore? Aren't I there?' Ramanan consoled Kamala.

Today there was an unusual rush in the Party Office. It had opened much before Ramanan opened his shop. Aaman Sir and Bhargavan, the Party Secretary, had reached there early. Several comrades had come in and gone out. Worry and anxiety were writ large on everyone's faces.

After the discussion, Aaman Sir came down into the midday heat.

'Drink a little cool water, please, Sir.'

Ramanan got up and bowed to him with folded palms as if he was Parassinikkadavu Muttappan himself.

'No.'

'A sarsaparilla sherbet?'

'There's no time for it, Ramanan.'

Before Ramanan could say anything more, Aaman Sir and the comrades began to walk on.

Ramanan had wanted to ask them for information about Appukkuttan.

Now, there is only Appukkuttan on everyone's lips. Everyone was relieved that Saravanan had croaked. And it was Appukkuttan who had done it.

'This locality has been purified,' said Moosath.

It was when he was thinking about Appukkuttan and pedalling his machine that Ramanan saw Ananthakrishnan crossing the road and coming towards him. Ramanan's legs became still.

Without paying attention to anyone, Ananthakrishnan went straight up to the Party Office.

As usual, on the long table in the middle of the room, newspapers and magazines were strewn about. Sitting on the benches were some youths, reading. There wasn't much of a rush, as it was around noon. The day's newspapers were lying there, awaiting readers.

Seeing the unexpected visitor, everyone was taken aback. A young man stood up and unfolded his tucked-in mundu in reverence. Others followed suit. It was not usual for anyone to show respect to Ananthakrishnan. Everyone only laughed at him. When he went to the temple for worship, or to make offerings, onlookers would privately scoff at him. Some would express their indignation:

'He is atoning for the sins he committed. That's why he is visiting temples like this. Doesn't he belong to the Party that beheaded people and put up their severed heads on the parapet of the gateway of the victims' houses? Those sins will not be absolved during a single lifetime. Let him suffer.'

Now, the youngsters seem to have forgotten the sins he committed and were standing up and paying him their respects.

'Isn't the Secretary here?'

'No.'

'Where has he gone?'

'To the police station, along with Aaman Sir.'

When he heard the word 'police station', Ananthakrishnan's face went pale. He swallowed hard. He had not yet gone there to see his son.

'Please have a seat.'

'Hey, you must tell me to lie down instead of offering me a seat. What I now need is not a chair but a mat.'

The youngsters stood around, not knowing what to say.

'I need a book.'

The Party Office doubles up as a reading room as well. In the old wooden almirahs full of termites, lined up along the walls, there are old books from Prabhat Book House and Chintha Publications.

'Which book?'

A young man picked up a key and stood before a shelf.

'*The Guinness Book*.'

The youth stared at Ananthakrishnan's face.

'*The Guinness Book of Records*. Haven't you heard of it?'

'No.' The young man said, somewhat uncertainly. He continued:

'It's not here. Any other book...'

'No. It's *The Guinness Book* that I need. If you haven't heard of it before, I'm telling you about it now. All the records of the world are entered in it. The fastest runner, the mother who has given birth the most times. Thus, all those who have created records are found in that book. It's a book all of us must read. Before long, the names of those who spit the longest shot of spittle after chewing betel and those who pass the longest jet of urine and so on will find a place in it.'

It was news for the young men. They asked themselves as to why Ananthakrishnan should need that book now. As if reading their mind, Ananthakrishnan said:

'I want to look up whether a fifteen-year-old boy has killed anyone before. Isn't it a great achievement if my Appu can find a place in *The Guinness Book*?'

Before the youngsters could say anything, Ananthakrishnan walked out.

As he walked on in the midday heat, the hem of his soiled mundu swept the ground. There were only a few people around. The coir factory owner, who was standing at the bus stop waiting for the bus, holding his open umbrella against the sun, looked away, turning his face as soon as he spotted Ananthakrishnan. Some shot him looks of derision. But the majority of the people felt sympathy for him.

That day, the Kannur editions of the leading newspapers had Appukkuttan's photo. Appukkuttan, who combed his hair like EMS and wore glasses, became well-known in a day. There was a crowd of news-reporters at Ananthakrishnan's house. They smothered him with questions. Ananthakrishnan sat looking at them, unable to speak a word, as if he had swallowed his own tongue. The *Malayala Manorama* reporter thought Ananthakrishnan had smiled faintly at them. On their way back, the reporters exchanged notes. *Mathrubhoomi*'s Ajayan too repeated that observation.

'He certainly did smile, looking at me. I've no doubt about it,' Prabhakaran said conclusively.

'You must just have imagined you saw him smile. How can any father smile on such an occasion?' *Maadhyamam*'s correspondent Ahmadkutty said.

'That's exactly what disturbs me. If Ananthakrishnan smiled at us, it's really very serious.'

'Shall we go back and see him once again?'

'No, Prabhakaran. That's no use at all. Let him be by himself for some time.'

But how can Ananthakrishnan get peace of mind?

From the previous day, the police, news-reporters and Partymen had been invading Ananthakrishan's house. Asianet's crew had come from Kozhikode during the night. They stood vigil in the courtyard, cameras poised. The camera, with its lone eye, captured everyone coming and going. In between, the cameraman, Sasidharan circled house once, the camera levelled on his shoulder. A press photographer got in through the kitchen and clicked away at Appukkuttan's books, pen, the chair he used to sit on to study, his shirt, and the armless vest hung from the line.

'How long have you been sitting like this, Ananthakrishnan? Come and eat at least a morsel of rice,' the old man of the neighbouring house said.

He had not kept up a healthy relationship with his neighbours. He wouldn't even acknowledge them when he met them. It was after a gap of so many years that the old man had set foot in his courtyard.

On the table inside were a tiffin carrier and a rolled-up plantain leaf. The food Aaman Sir had sent from the Party Office. Ananthakrishnan didn't touch it. Although he hadn't drunk even a drop of water that day, he didn't feel hungry or thirsty.

By evening, the rush in Ananthakrishnan's house had dwindled. One after another, newsmen, photographers and TV crews left the scene. The lamp was neglected to be lit, darkness rushed in.

Like the hero of a B-grade movie, Appukkuttan sat holding the iron bars of the police lock-up, his eyes raised to the sky. He felt that the sky was unusually far away. Among the stars that were scattered in the clear sky, he recognised the red star, and, as he looked on, that star's glow increased and a pair of spectacle-lenses formed before him. Appukkuttan looked on, holding his breath, as that star metamorphosed into EMS's face. The flow of light from that star extended into Appukkuttan's cell, and along that red ray, EMS came walking down. EMS—with the same glasses, the same face and the same childlike smile, as he saw in the picture kept for sale in the stall during Mathappura Muttappan's festival—came and stood before Appukkuttan and then entered the lock-up enveloped by the red light. Appukkuttan fell forward into the white-haired, dark hands of EMS. Until dawn, those hands kept gently stroking Appukkuttan's head.

Thirty-one

I believe it is proper to state here a serious disagreement between Kesavan and myself, before I evaluate Kesavan's latest novel, *Appukkuttan*'s *Lamentations*, which ran into a second edition within three weeks of publication. Let me make it clear that it is not to lend objectivity to my study of the novel by negating the friendship that exists between Kesavan and myself, that I make this statement here. We know that it is not the friendship between the novelist and the critic that deepens the creative engagement between the two. It is the orgasmic point of dissent that makes the reciprocity between the creator and critic possible. It is because they are able to recognise this as a fact that certain creators and critics manage to develop the creativity of dissent, transcending the boundaries of the personal.

When he was addressing the post-graduate students of the Malayalam Department of a college a few months ago, Kesavan repeatedly stressed the necessity to view one's life and creative works as two strictly separate domains. Even earlier, he exhibited glimmers of this idea on certain occasions. We have to specially note the fact that Kesavan is not attempting to theorise but merely developing this idea connecting to certain incidents of his own life. It is but a basic notion that any idea connected to committed literature would slide into subjectivity, if not buttressed by theory. When Kesavan says that he must keep his everyday life away from the world of his writing, it is a position he takes against subjectivity. Thus, when he takes positions for and against subjectivity in a single idea, I don't think it points to defective thinking.

Kesavan's thinking has always been dialectical. The gaps between his thoughts and actions are developing as a hallmark of his creativity.

My disagreement with Kesavan has mainly to do with the above-noted absence of an emotional bond between the creator and the creation, which Kesavan tries to justify through his arguments. It is not easy to establish that a literary creation can take birth in an absence like that. The creation of a literary work becomes possible when the author, leaning firmly on to the emotional bent of mind of a society, makes interventions in its political or historical spaces. A creative writer must never attempt to dispense with emotions and engage in discourses in the academic sphere.

But, as pointed out earlier, Kesavan's world of ideas is a composite world of contradictions. The character of that world has the chaotic nature of dreams rather than the adamantine firmness of reason. Kesavan is a writer who slides and slithers away like a catfish, without yielding access to any critic.

It is a writer who is totally different from this Kesavan that I see in *Appukkuttan's Lamentations*. In this novel we see Kesavan —who had hitherto exhibited misgivings and dissent during his creative experience spanning the last two decades—bravely taking up the pen, wielding immense self-confidence and clarity. This is why I recognise *Appukkuttan's Lamentations* as a turning point in the creative life of this writer. Although I have not yet examined in detail the vision illuminated in this novel, as also strategies of technique, I do not require the comfort of a second thought to declare that this is the most well-crafted and substantial among all the novels of Kesavan.

The most prominent among the accusations shot relentlessly at Kesavan by literary enthusiasts and critics, concerns the apolitical nature of his works. He never cared either to refute them or to argue with his critics on this count. Just as he always separated his private life from his works, he also saw criticism and accusations as separate from his works. He has never been seen coming forward to communicate with, or to have an interface with, other writers or literary critics. Yet, I always had misgivings about Kesavan's apolitical stance. Kesavan always considered the accusation of apoliticality a boon and strove to develop his silence behind it. It is, however, not very difficult for those who know Kesavan intimately to note that it was one of the many ruses Kesavan employed to ensure the 'naturalness' of his novels and stories and for his survival on the literary scene.

When I learned that Kesavan was going to write a novel about EMS, many a doubt came into my mind. I was really concerned. I had feared that it would be the most dangerous adventure of Kesavan's writing life, and that it would finally be his suicide as a writer.

In order to write about a personality like EMS, whom I would like to describe as 'The Most Enlightened Malayalee of This Century', one requires a deep sense of history and a mature political sense. It is obvious from his other writings that

Kesavan's is a mind that refuses to communicate with history. This writer, who never attempts to enter the world outside his novels and stories and engage in normal communication, can here be seen throwing to the outside world some of his own observations through the mouth of his characters. Against this backdrop, I recall the words of Bishambaran in *Bharatamata*: 'I am not returning to Jagatpur. The narrow streets of that place, raising dust even at midnight, triggering memories of communal riots, are alien to me.'

It was because I knew that Kesavan lacked the sense of history and political maturity required to write about a leader of the millennium like EMS, that I grew anxious over his new venture and even took the extreme step of forewarning him. Kesavan is a creative writer, through and through. It is but elementary that creativity alone is insufficient to write a novel, with EMS—an ever-expanding presence in history, the Bhishmacharya of the political Kurukshetra—as the central character.

But let me record here with pleasure that the very first reading of *Appukkuttan's Lamentations* erased all the anxieties and misgivings in me. As soon as I finished reading and shut the book, I recognised my misgivings turning into consolation and anxieties, to rejoicing.

Kesavan establishes, through *Appukkuttan's Lamentations*, that there are so many ways open to a writer to approach EMS and the ideological premises he represents, without establishing the exteriority of a historical position. The view through the eyes of a child is one of them. I realise that it was quite improper on my part to suspect that the adoption of this path was a ruse thought up by Kesavan to keep himself away from historical and political responsibility, thus availing himself an anticipatory bail as well.

As soon as he employs this method of creating the narrative from a child's perspective, Kesavan breaks away from all traditional modes. When we realise that what Kesavan achieves, as he views our contemporary political history through the innocent eyes of a child, is not the rejection of history, but the rejection, instead, of the exteriorisation of history, we are able to read *Appukkuttan's Lamentations* through its multiple layers of meaning. And, at the same time, Kesavan sabotages our notion that the viewpoint of a child implies freedom from all prejudices. The purity of vision is also an intervention. What Kesavan does is, problematise our political conditions, hiding behind the innocence and simplicity of the perspective of the boy, Appukkuttan. This is just one of the strategies Kesavan always used at the level of ideas and writing. Whatever the strategies he employs, the final set of meanings *Appukkuttan's Lamentations* generates is progressive. This is why I believe that, though it is a novel that could potentially become the author's literary suicide, it remains at the pinnacle his achievement, as a beacon illuminating our social-historical-political spheres.

Here, I remember a painting by Jamini Roy, *The Queen Sitting Atop a Tiger*. It was the child in Jamini Roy who painted this picture. With this one piece, he rejuvenated modern painting, which was nearing its death through the blows dealt to it by the polyphony of colours and complexity of art. There is a child hidden in every creator. When the creation is filled with complexity, this child comes out and purifies the creation.

What Kesavan achieves through the child Appukkuttan is the purification of our fiction. Therefore, I recognise and uphold

Appukkuttan's Lamentations as a major work, not only of Kesavan, but of the contemporary fiction of our language…

(Excerpts from the study published in two consecutive issues of *Keralam Weekly*).

Thirty-two

'Haven't you finished writing the novel? Let's now go somewhere. Haven't you been working so hard without even eating and drinking?'

'All right. Let's go. But where'll we go?'

Kesavan looked at his wife helplessly, as if there was no place to go in a country as big as ours.

'Let's go to see the Malampuzha Dam.'

Since the day they had been married, she had been asking him for just this. It was a wish that had taken root in Sujatha's mind in her childhood. When she was studying in class eight, all the students of the class and the teachers had gone on an excursion to Malampuzha. Because of a sudden bout of diarrhoea and vomiting, Sujatha had not been able to go along with them. The wish to go to Malampuzha attached itself to her mind even now, like the sticky sap of jackfruit.

'What right does man have to block the course of rivers? The flow of rivers should not be obstructed. No one goes on a picnic to see flowing rivers. Everyone wants to see blocked-up rivers.'

'I don't want to listen to your Vedanta. Hasn't it been quite some time since I have been listening to this? Take Satheesan and me along to see Malampuzha. Don't raise lame excuses,' Sujatha said, darkly.

It was Sujatha who was elated and more relieved than Kesavan when he finished the novel. Whenever he took up the pen, it sowed discomfort in the house. When he paced up and down the house all night with all lights on, when he came back from the bathroom where he had locked himself up with soap and towel but without having a bath, when he refused to come out of the toilet, when he sat not uttering a word when guests had come visiting, when he spanked Satheesan without any reason and when he poked cruel fun at their neighbour, the young unemployed Aravindan, Sujatha would silently pray to Parassinikkadavu Muttappan, urging him not to make Kesavan write another novel. And immediately seek Muttappan's pardon as well, feeling guilty about making such a wish.

'All right. Let's go to see the Malampuzha Dam.'

'Swear, placing your palm on my head.'

'Not merely on your head, I shall swear, touching you all over your body.'

He did swear, touching each of limbs from head to foot.

'If you do not take me to Malampuzha now, I'll die. Didn't you promise, touching my head?'

'I'll die before you do. Just wait and see.'

'Is it we who decide who will die first? Everything will happen as Muttappan decides.'

After two days, carrying an old airbag, Kesavan, Sujatha and Satheesan boarded the Madras Mail, travelling towards Palakkad. From Palakkad, by bus and by taxi they reached the Malampuzha Dam.

Those were the happiest three days of Sujatha's life. They roamed around in Palakkad town till their legs gave way. When they felt thirsty they drank lemonade and when hungry they ate at restaurants. And slept in the lodging house at night, oblivious of everything. When they were about to return, he bought a silk saree and a pair of sandals for her. The return journey was by the Mangalore Mail.

'Life is beautiful, isn't it, Kesavetta?' she said, sitting in the train. Looking at the paddy fields, coconut groves and plantain groves, she dozed off.

Sujatha's happiness didn't escape his notice. Now he doesn't harbour the guilt that he has never given her any happiness. He believes that happiness is not given by someone and that it has to be discovered by oneself. If the trip to Malampuzha had remained with her till now as an unfulfilled wish, what had she been waiting for, for so long? If he didn't take her along, couldn't she have taken him along, instead? Musing thus, Kesavan sat in the verandah.

There comes, then, Ravunni, Unni Kurup and Pavithran. Behind them is a woman in churidar-kurta.

'Hey, where did you go? We have been roaming around your house since yesterday,' Ravunni said, as soon as he spotted Kesavan from afar. His tummy bulges out more now. Is it undigested ideology or brandy that's in it?

'We went sightseeing to the Malampuzha Dam. We have come back only just now, by the Mangalore Mail,' Sujatha said from the doorway. Pavithran's wife Ganga moved over to her side and stood holding her hands.

'Sujatha, three glasses, please.'

'Four.'

Ravunni looked up at Kesavan with misgivings. The faces of Pavithran and Unni Kurup brightened instantly. The kind of happiness that one feels when one finds some money lying on the roadside, could be seen on their faces. Their only worry was whether the money was genuine currency or fake and the urgency to confirm the truth was palpable. Ravunni's suspicion soon faded. He felt that this, too, was one of Kesavan's jokes. He had played so many of them, in place and out of place.

'Didn't you see Ravunni Master's critical piece?'

'What critical piece?'

'Indeed!' Pavithran was incredulous. 'Haven't you seen the last two numbers of *Keralam Weekly*?'

'No.'

'That article has been a hot topic of discussion among lovers of literature. Everyone is talking about it. And yet haven't you read it? Or even seen it?'

'Kesavan, Pavithran is talking about the article Ravunni Master wrote about *Lamentations of Appukkuttan,*' Unni Kurup explained. '"The Purity of Vision".'

It was a study of his own work. It was written, moreover, by a critic as prominent as Ravunni. Yet, Kesavan didn't feel bad about not having seen it. Kesavan doesn't read any criticism or study of his own work.

He believes that reading them serves him no purpose.

'I know your habits.'

Ravunni pulled out two issues of *Keralam Weekly* from his shoulder bag. 'Read. And tell me whether you agree with me or not.'

Kesavan took the magazines. On the cover of the first one, on the right hand top corner, there was a small photo of EMS.

Below, to the left, a large colour photo of Kesavan. On one side of Kesavan's photo, there was a headline in block letters against a red background…

'Father called him Appu, Mother called him Kuttan. And the people called him Appukkuttan.'

Kesavan felt a cloying sensation as he read the sentences. He feared that he would throw up if he read that line again. Kesavan handed back the weekly to Ravunni. Ravunni didn't take it back. He had payed twelve rupees to buy it for Kesavan.

'Doesn't the *Keralam Weekly* send you complimentary copies?' asked Pavithran. 'I remember seeing its copies in your room some time ago.'

Pavithran had a sharp memory. From its very inception, *Keralam Weekly* had sent complimentary copies to Kesavan. Recently the editor had written to Kesavan asking for his opinion about the weekly, had Kesavan replied. How was he to comment on a weekly he never read? Ever since, his complimentary copies had stopped coming. Kesavan had not disclosed this to Pavithran, Unni Kurup or Ravunni. Most of Ravunni's heavyweight articles used to come out in *Keralam*.

Sujatha set down four glasses in front of them. The fourth glass was taller than the other three. At one first glance, it reminded one of Moosath. The other three were short and rotund. They reminded one of Visalakshi Ezhuthamma. As Sujatha walked back after placing the three Visalakshi Ezhuthammas and one Moosath on the bench, Ravunni called out from behind, 'Sujatha, stop. Let me tell you something.'

'Is it something private? Then come inside and tell me.'

'It's certainly something private. But take it as a private thing to be heard by all present now. It's about your husband.

What sort of a person is this Kesavan of yours? Within four weeks of his new novel coming out, I wrote a study on thirty foolscap pages. It was published in two issues of the best weekly in Malayalam. It came out as a cover story because I spoke to the editor about it. It even had Kesavan's photo on the cover page. Do not think that I am speaking about it because I wrote it. Everyone is talking about it. And yet, your husband doesn't even know that I have written such an article. Never mind. Paying twelve rupees, I bought both the issues of the weekly and gave it to him. Yet, he didn't even open it. What kind of a man is he? How do you live with him, Sujatha?'

'Kesavettan is such a loving person. He took me and Satheesan on a sightseeing trip to Malampuzha dam.'

Pavithran held the three Visalakshi Ezhuthammas upside down, draining the little water that lingered in them, and poured brandy into their mouths. Then he added water.

'Pour some into the mouth of Moosath as well.' Kesavan proffered his glass.

'No Pavithran. He won't drink. He will pour it under the table when we are not looking,' Ravunni said. He continued, 'Rum and brandy are too expensive. Let the prices go up; from now on, it won't affect me. The Party will give me a ticket for the next election. With that, I'll stop drinking and become a good Communist.'

'You can't become a good Communist merely by mending your drinking habits. You have to starve as well.'

Kesavan took the bottle and poured brandy into his own glass. The pungent smell of brandy hit his nostrils and his eyes smarted.

'What brandy is this? Is it distilled from fire?' Kesavan asked himself.

'Cheers.'

Unni Kurup kissed Kesavan's glass with his own. He was very glad that Kesavan had joined them at long last. When Ravunni had set off to Kesavan's house with a bottle in his shoulder bag, Unni Kurup had forbidden him. What fun was there in drinking sitting in the house of someone who doesn't drink, join the company of friends, or even talk to them? Unni Kurup had asked.

The Visalakshi Ezhuthammas in Ravunni's and Pavithran's hands pecked Moosath on both cheeks and then gave him deep, lingering kisses.

It was Ravunni who emptied his glass first. Kesavan came second, Unni Kurup third and Pavithran fourth. Pavithran senses that his craze for drink is on the downslide after marriage.

'Kesavan, I too have certain things to tell you. You can take it as a complaint, if you like. You saw that girl clad in a churidar, who stood in front of you a little while ago? So you can't pretend any more that you haven't come to know that I have got married. And yet, did you so much as speak a word to her? She came to your house for the first time. When the wedding invitations were printed, it's to you I sent the first one. Anticipating the possibility that you may even go to the extent of claiming that that card which I personally posted didn't reach you, I met you personally and handed over a card. Fearing that you would even deny that fact, it was in Sujatha's presence as witness that I handed over that card to you. And then? Even then, you didn't come for my wedding. You told Unni Kurup that you forgot. And to Ravunni Master, you said you couldn't get leave because of the busy work in your office. You have no love for friends. You don't have love towards anyone. Not even for yourself.'

Kesavan sat looking into the glass, as if into a volcano. It seemed as if the fire, smoke and lava inside the glass were reflecting on his face.

'Kesavan. I too have a complaint,' Unni Kurup licked his lips wet with brandy. 'Yours is a rock-hard mind. What did you tell some college students, who were members of our Party, when they came to you for fund-raising? You told them to bring along their pretty sisters if any, and that you would then give them a handsome donation. You insulted them so harshly and sent them away. You spoke to them in a kind of language a litterateur should never use. They know that you are our friend. That's the only reason why they didn't leave with your head in their hands. Kesava, you are writing a novel about our leader. And when our boys come to you for a donation, you shower them with obscenities. What logic is there in it?'

'Pour a drop more,' said Kesavan.

Pavithran poured the remaining brandy into Kesavan's glass. Kesavan sat savouring it with relish. Each time he put the glass to his lips, he felt anxious that the brandy in it would soon be finished. He darted frequent envious glances towards Pavithran's full glass. When his glass was empty, he waited cunningly to snatch Pavithran's glass away from his hand.

Thirty-three

Kesavan heaved himself up on his hands, and walked towards the door, holding on to chairs and benches for support. When he wound the mundu tightly, leaning against the door, the coins tucked inside scattered on the floor. Seeing a twenty-five paise coin rolling away and suddenly splitting in two and running off in opposite directions, he was bewildered.

'Be careful when you cross the street. Don't wait for a bus. Hire an autorickshaw and go home straight.' Chirukandan said.

When Kesavan had reached there in the morning, Chirukandan had not paid any attention to him at all. He had talked to him as coarsely as he did to other customers. Most of his customers were labourers who worked in the godowns and jetties. With sun-burned and weather-beaten faces, they come there for cheap liquor. Drinking cheap brandy or whisky, filling themselves to the brim with rice and meat curry, they leave only after handing over to Chirukandan the lion's share of their daily wages.

'Hello there, buy yourself some green-gram or chickpea curry; otherwise, this liquor will burn up your bowels.' Advised a labourer sitting next to Kesavan, watching him drinking brandy on an empty stomach, without any snacks on the side. His breath reeked of dried fish and bidi.

'Chirukandan Modalaly, give him something to eat.'

'What do you want to eat?' Chirukandan asked him, yet again. Kesavan didn't reply. He was observing the tiny bubbles climbing the sides of the glass of brandy into which soda had been poured.

Although the labourer sitting next to him tried several times to talk to Kesavan, he finally picked up his glass and pewter plate and moved over to the next table when not a single word was uttered in response.

'O my God, who's this? Isn't it our Kesavan Master? I can't believe my eyes. How'd you come here, Master?'

A bearded youngster who had just entered, stood aghast. Then he walked up to Kesavan and stood there deferentially, unable to decide whether to sit or stand, as if his feet were glued to the ground. It took him some time to regain his balance.

'Chirukandan Modalaly, d'you know who is sitting here?'

'He is drinking without touching even a few snacks. Won't his intestines burn up?'

'O my Modalaly, this is Kesavan Master. The real Kesavan Master who wrote the novel about EMS.'

At the mention of EMS, the heads of the drinking labourers spun towards Kesavan. A labourer pumped his fist into the air and shouted:

Long Live the Revolution!
Long Live Martyrs!

The young man loaded and unloaded salt in Ahamad Haji's godown.

'Is yesterday's paper lying here?'

'It's there.'

The bearded young man scanned the heap of papers lying on the packing cases and extracted the previous day's paper.

'Here, Chirukandan Modalaly, look.'

In the paper the young man held up, there was Kesavan's photo, filling three columns. Incredulous, Chirukandan looked at the picture and then at Kesavan's face, repeatedly. Forgetting their glasses, the labourers of the godown and jetty also sat staring at Kesavan. Two people who were sitting in a far corner came over and asked the bearded one, 'Young man, who is this Master? I've seen this Master somewhere.'

'This is Kesavan Master,' the youngster repeated. 'Kesavan, who writes stories and novels.'

Looking at Kesavan with new respect and whispering among themselves, they took up the glasses from the table once again.

'What do you want?'

'Let it be some expensive brand. Is it a small thing to have a drink with Kesavan Master? This is my great luck. Modalaly, can we get a photographer?'

Although Kesavan was listening to everything, he sat sipping brandy oblivious to it all. A sea breeze was blowing in through the window from time to time. Sometimes the breeze came in from the open, sooty window shutters of the kitchen. The pungent odour of the fish curry permeated the air around.

The youngster sat beside Kesavan and continued chatting as if he was an old pal. It seemed that he was talking only to himself. Not a word issued from Kesavan's mouth. He didn't answer even a single question. The youngster felt very disappointed. After a while, he also slipped into silence. They sat side by side and went on drinking.

When he felt that he had had enough, Kesavan heaved himself up on his elbows, walked past the drinking labourers and left. At the end of the road leading to the jetty, a big stretch of sea glimmered. Turning his back toward the sea, Kesavan walked to the main road. The sight of tall, ancient buildings, hand carts carrying bags of grain, and the godowns, gave Kesavan the impression that he was in Mattancherry. He had gone to Fort Kochi years ago. Nursing this old memory, Kesavan walked past Ahamad Haji's godown and reached the main road. Discarding Chirukandan's advice, he walked among the hand-carts and lorries loaded with different wares. On both sides were godowns and wholesale depots. When he passed different shops, the scents of ginger, pepper, gingelli oil and washing soap pierced his nostrils. Although honking autos came close, grazing him and inviting him, he didn't get into any of them. He walked on till his legs ached. When he felt that he could not go on any more, he got into the Town Bus and stood holding on to the handbar on the roof. He resolved that as soon as he reached home he would eat his fill, open all the windows of his room, lie on his cot and sleep as long as he wanted to. Holding on to the hand-bar, slid into deep sleep. Even his sub-conscious mind had begun to sleep.

'What's it, are you sleeping standing up? May I spread a mat for you?'

'It's doomsday! People have even begun to sleep standing up.'

'He wouldn't have got time to sleep at night.'

In response to that jibe, all those who were standing around Kesavan laughed. The women turned their faces away and stared outside. Kesavan didn't notice any of this. His hold on the top hand-bar loosened. The other passengers were supporting him now.

'This guy is completely sozzled. Who else can sleep like this? Usually people drink after coming back from work. Nowadays, people go to the liquor shop early in the morning. There's a time for everything. And there should be a time for drinking too. Or else, if this lot go about drinking all the time, gentlemen will not be able to walk about. Or travel in a bus, for that matter. There should be some law for all this. But the government that is supposed to make laws pretends that nothing's wrong. What is it to the government even if the people drink poison? They need only the tax collected on the sale of toddy, arrack and liquor. Nowadays, governance is big business. Ministers are excellent merchants. How then is the lot of the country going to improve? We can only suffer.'

Kesavan didn't hear what the old man said.

Kesavan wasn't aware of the bus turning bends, braking, passengers falling on to his body or people getting in and out.

Finally, when the bus reached the junction, Kesavan got down. Waking from sleep, he looked around and yawned. Like Saravanan, the character he had created, he began to pee by the roadside.He didn't see anyone on the scorched street. But the paan shop owner Nanootty and teashop owner Kannan came running towards him. They seemed to have been waiting for him. Amazement was writ large on their faces, as if they were meeting him for the first time after many years.

'You know who's been to your house? Go quickly.'

'Nanootty, give me your bicycle. I'll take Master on its carrier.'

'I know the way to my own house,'said Kesavan.

On the roadside, there was an old Ambassador parked at the point where the lane branched off. The day's *Deshaabhimaani* paper was lying in its backseat.

He couldn't wait to reach his house and just collapse on the bed. Kesavan was totally spent.

Loud slogan-shouting rose from the lane.

Long Live Eeyyemmes!
Long Live Martyrs!
Long Live the Revolution!

When Kesavan was spotted coming towards them, walking as if on someone else's legs, someone shouted from the crowd:

Long Live Kesavan!
Go on writing, writing,
With courage, courage!

As in the lane below, there were people crowding his courtyard as well. As Kesavan climbed the hewn steps, stepped over the wicker gate and reached the courtyard, Ravunni came running to him. What would a person who wore glasses, look like without them? That's how Kesavan saw EMS. Is that the EMS I created in *Appukkuttan's Lamentations*? Or the real EMS? Kesavan couldn't distinguish between the two.

A smile spread on EMS's face. A tooth on the right side of his jaw was chipped. There was a boil on his skin on the neck just below the chin. Kesavan bent over, touched those dark feet smeared with mud. EMS bent slightly forward and raised his right hand. The onlookers couldn't understand whether it was to bless him or to prevent Kesavan from touching his feet that EMS did so.

'I've read it,' said EMS. 'I like it.'

'Eeyyemmes is going to write about it in detail in the next issue of *Deshaabhimaani,*' Ravunni informed him.

EMS spent half-an-hour in Kesavan's house. Before leaving, he placed his palm on Sujatha's head in benediction. With Ravunni's support, he got out into the courtyard and made his way through the crowd of the people. The crowd followed him, shouting slogans. By this time, Kesavan's locality had woken up. In front of houses, on embankments and by the roadside, people had gathered. All faces showed excitement and elation.

Ravunni got into the car with EMS and sat next to him. As the car moved away, children ran after it. People lined up along both sides of the road, and raised slogans. Some were carrying red flags. Even after EMS's car had disappeared into the distance, they kept on waving the flags. Even as he stood watching all these, there remained that doubt in Kesavan's mind—was it the real EMS? Or was he the EMS whom he had depicted on white paper in red ink?

Kesavan didn't go back to his house. He walked forward along the road where crowd had walked. Having lost the capacity of his hands and legs, he moved on like a puppet. Although he tried to raise his hands requesting the passing buses to stop, his hand couldn't be raised....

When he got down from the bus and walked forward among the godowns, the jetty was glowing red on the face of the road.

Seeing Kesavan returning, Chirukandan felt uncomfortable. As it was dusk, labourers were coming in, in large numbers. Within no time, there was hardly any place to sit. Kesavan looked at everyone's face, in a daze like a moron. Kesavan, the intellectual, had turned a halfwit within the space of a day. Chirukandan Modalaly personally brought the brandy and soda Kesavan had ordered and placed it before him. Holding the washed glass against the burning bulb, he examined whether it was properly cleaned.

The labourers sitting around began to talk aloud, sing and raise a din. It seemed that each one was talking not for others to hear, but only for oneself.

'That devil Abootty has swindled me of the two thousand and five hundred rupees which I earned doing dog's work. When he said it was for the remarriage of his divorced daughter and touched my feet, begging for help, I gave it to him without a second thought. Who could then think that he would cheat me? Lucky for him that he is an old man. If not, I'd have broken his ribs.'

The labourer who had been cheated of his money took out a beedi, tossed it towards his mouth, caught it between his teeth, lit it and drew on it and blew out the smoke forcefully.

Another labourer, who wore a rudrakshamala around his neck, also had a tale of treachery to relate.

'That daughter of Kayat Chaattu betrayed me. It was for her that I did hard labour work, rain or shine, in the jetty. She had sworn an oath touching her heart that she wouldn't marry any one else but me.Who has bought for her the black-bead-studded gold necklace she wore for the festival of Andaloorkkavu? I bought it with the money I got by discounting at considerable loss a monthly chitfund of the face value of rupees 8000. When my sisters go to school soaked in rain, have I given them at least an umbrella? Does my father have some Ayurvedic oil to rub on his back when he gets that bad backache? Does my mother have a blanket to cover herself with on cold nights? Do I have a clean mundu or shirt to change into in the evenings, after my work? She has wrecked it all. That daughter of Chaattu. She'll be damned. My flesh revolts when I see her going about draped in a Nylex sari, together with that Dubai-wallah. Damn her. Doesn't he come flying over the sea? I have vowed a Vellattu for Parassinikkadavu Muttappan. His plane will drop into the sea and he will be drowned. That's for certain.'

He poured into his mouth the ounce of rum that remained in the glass, and put the chilli chutney on his tongue.

Listening to the tales of betrayal the labourers were recounting, Kesavan drank up three-fourths of a pint of brandy. He felt as if he heard a plane plunge into the sea. Parassinnikkadavu Muttappan must have heard the betrayed labourer's plea. He sat looking at the brandy that remained in the bottle. Enough, he said to himself. I can't drink anymore. He called over Chirukandan Modalaly, paid his bill and got up to leave.

'Walk carefully,' Chirukandan Modalaly advised him.

As he walked along the road to the jetty, enjoying the sea breeze, he was certain that he wouldn't be able to reach home that night and that he would have to lie down somewhere outside one of the godowns till morning. The godowns and shops were shut. When the lights went out in the buildings, the road was plunged in darkness. Traffic had almost ceased.

There was busy traffic only in the sky. Clouds blown about by the winds created traffic jams there. There was not even a traffic policeman around to control the traffic of clouds. As he walked on with the dust of the jetty on his feet, the first raindrops fell.

As he walked along, the alley turned dark because the streetlights had gone out, his foot caught the end of his mundu, and he tottered. There was light only in Kesavan's house, like a candle that shone burning away in darkness. He felt that his house was really far away and that he wouldn't reach there even if he were to walk throughout the night. He stood for some time, holding on to the embankment for support. For a moment a torch flashed on top of the embankment and some people came running down. With the hope that they would take him to his house, he waited for them to come closer....

Kesavan could laugh on certain occasions, when others couldn't even think of laughing. That's why the axe* that descended on him in the dark paused for a second, hearing his laughter. Only for a second....

---

* The axe symbolises the RSS-Marxist conflicts in Kannur region that have claimed many innocent lives.

Glossary

Ankanam Award: A literary award meant for Malayalam writers under forty.

Blade Company: Private financial institutions which mushroomed all over Kerala especially during the Seventies and Eighties, which were notorious for their extortionately high rates of interest (hence 'blade'), and the unscrupulous methods they employed in recovering bad debts.

Chedathi: Honorific address for a woman, especially a Christian, who is senior to the person addressing, either by age or rank.

Choroonu: The ritual first feeding of rice to an infant, often carried out in front of a deity in a special temple like the one in Guruvayoor.

Chukkuvellam: Ginger-water.

Ellunda: A sweet; it is a ball made of fried sesame seeds dipped in jaggery-syrup.

Erisserry: A vegetable curry made using mainly elephant foot yam, raw banana, pumpkin, string beans, garlic, chilly, curry leaves etc., cooked in coconut gravy and topped with fried grated coconut.

Ezhuthamma: In the north Malabar parlance, a teacher, usually in primary school.

Japa: The ritually repeated chanting of mantras, keeping the count on stringed beads.

Jayan and Ranichandra: Malayalam celluloid idols of yore; incidentally, both died in accidents.

Kaiser: A typical name given to dogs in Kerala; the British colonisers must have first used this name of the villain of World War I on their pet male dogs, following which the colonial subjects named their male dogs likewise.

Kanji: Rice gruel.

Kanjivellam: Rice-water.

Kashayam: An Ayurvedic concoction of medicinal extracts, prepared through a process of repeated boiling of herbs in particular measures of water.

Kunnikkuru: The pink, black-headed seed of *Abrus Precatorius*, traditionally used as a unit of weight in weighing gold; children gather them to play with, or to make garlands out of them.

Mundu: The long loin cloth that is wound around the waist, reaching down to one's ankles.

Murikku: The coral tree, with thorny trunk, and bright red flowers.

Muttathu Varkey Award: A prestigious Malayalam literary award, instituted in the name of a writer of popular fiction, which has hitherto been won by several critically acclaimed writers of Malayalam fiction.

Nilavilakku: A tall bronze lamp, with an open dish-like upper portion with several slots all around its brim for wicks to rest and in which coconut oil is filled; used in temples, homes, on stage in ritual performances like Kathakali, Koodiyattam, Koothu, in inaugural ceremonies etc.

Ossan: A barber exclusively for Muslims, who also carries out the ritual of circumcision.

Paara: A sturdy spear-like implement used to husk coconut; often made of thick areca nut-tree wood or palm-wood; has a double meaning in local parlance, as 'a person who causes wilful trouble for others'.

Payankutty: A form of offering for Muttappan, the ancestor-god worshipped at Parassinikkadavu, near Taliparambu, north Malabar.

Prasad:	The portion of the offering given back to the devotee after it has been offered to the deity by the priest.
Pulpalli:	A place in Wynad district of Kerala, where one of the first Naxalite assaults on a police camp took place in 1968.
Sarkkari:	Typically, the lower-rung bureaucratic class.
Sarsaparilla:	A medicinal root-tuber; *Hemidesmus Cordatus* or *Periploca Indica.*
Sattvic:	One who possesses the quality of sattva, or immovable clarity of consciousness
Sree Narayana Dharma Paripalana Sangam:	An organisation for social reformation formed by the great seer-reformer of Kerala, Sree Narayana Guru, in the early twentieth century
Thannirpandal:	A little shack by the roadside where cool water is kept in huge earthen pots for the benefit of thirsty wayfarers in summer.
Thoran:	A dry side-dish for a lunch or dinner of a main rice course; prepared using finely cut vegetable with half-ground coconut, garlic, chilly, cumin seed etc.